TOMAS

DE LA VEGA FAMILIA TRILOGY

DAWN SULLIVAN

Published by: Dawn Sullivan

Cover Design: Sweet 15 Designs

Editor: Ryder Editing and Formatting

Copyright 2021 © Author Dawn Sullivan

Language: English

TOMAS

As the eldest son of Miguel De La Vega, Tomas should have been next in line to lead the family's crime syndicate. As the bastard child of the Don's deceased mistress, the opportunity would pass him by. It didn't matter to him. It kept him out of the spotlight. He preferred being the muscle, taking care of business with his fists or his guns. Let one of his brothers worry about the political side of their corrupt business, and he would clean up their mess. Tomas was damn good at what he did, and everyone knew it.

Salome Villanueva was on the run from the one person she should have been able to trust in life… her own father. He'd made a deal with the devil, and she was the payment. Screw that. She wasn't some whimpering female quaking in her heels. She was strong, independent, and once she knew exactly who was after her besides her own family, she was going to turn the tables on them and show them a hell they would never have imagined. Until then, she would ask for help from the only people she knew of who could protect her. The mafia.

The moment Tomas set eyes on the fiery woman, he knew he was going to make Salome his. Salome had more important things to worry about than falling for a De La Vega, no matter how much she might want him. When her enemies get closer, Tomas will do everything in his power to save her, even if it means losing his own life in the process.

PROLOGUE

"Get under the bed, Tomas! Hurry!"

Tomas frowned, looking up as his mother ran into her bedroom, where he was sitting in the middle of the floor playing with a toy car.

"Do it!" she ordered, pointing to her bed, her dark brown eyes full of fear.

"But why, Mamá? I want to see Papá when he comes."

His mother knelt on the floor next to him, cupping his cheeks in her hands as she whispered, "Your Papá will be here later, Mijo. For now, you must hide."

Tomas jumped when there was a loud banging noise from the front of their small apartment, and then a crash.

"We are out of time, my sweet boy," his mother said hoarsely, grabbing him close and placing a hard kiss on his cheek. "You must listen now. Just like we practiced. Get under the bed and don't come out until you hear your Papá's voice."

"Mamá!" Tomas cried, reaching for her in terror when there was another loud crash.

"Be strong, Tomas," his mother whispered, picking him up and rushing across the room with him. "Stay very quiet. No matter what, you stay hidden and don't make a sound." Her eyes filled with tears as she gave him one last hug. "I love you so much, Mijo."

She had just slid him under the bed, making sure the comforter touched the floor, hiding him from sight, when a voice rang out loudly in the apartment.

"Antonela Cortes, you filthy little bitch!"

Tomas huddled under the bed, clutching his toy tightly in his little fist, his eyes wide as he listened.

"Diego, please, don't!"

"Sleeping with our sworn enemy?"

"No, I wouldn't!"

"You lie!"

There was a loud sound, and his mother screamed. Tomas couldn't help it. He knew he was supposed to stay hidden under the bed; they'd gone through this same scenario before several times when his mother felt he might be in danger, but tonight was different. Tonight was the first time he actually felt as if something bad was going to happen. He had to see what was going on.

"Where is your son, Antonela?"

"Away," his mother sobbed.

"We've checked the other rooms," another voice cut in. "There's no sign of him."

"I told you," his mother cried, "he isn't here!"

"Whose is he?" the one called Diego demanded.

"He's mine!"

Tomas grasped the bottom of the comforter with his little fingers and lifted it up just enough so he could peek out from under it. He saw his mother's feet in the pretty, light blue slippers she always wore in the house. Beside her were a large pair of shoes, so big he thought for sure the guy had to be a giant like in the story his mamá read him at night.

"His father, Antonela. Who is his father?"

"Why are you doing this, Diego?" his mother asked, and Tomas watched as her feet moved back toward him slightly. "You know who his father is."

Tomas held his breath, holding in the sobs that wanted to escape. He didn't know who this Diego person was, but the man terrified him. His voice was rough, mean, and full of anger.

"Do I?" Diego snarled. "I thought it was my cousin, Samuel, but I'm beginning to wonder. Remind me. How old is he now? Four? Five?"

"He's five," his mother gasped. "Just a child."

Tomas raised the comforter a little more, and then couldn't stop himself from raising it even higher. It revealed the man's legs, then his chest, and finally, his face. The cold, hard mask made Tomas gulp, his grip on the comforter tightening even more.

"Samuel died five years ago," Diego said, reaching out and grabbing a hand full of Antonela's dark hair, yanking her head back. "It would be easy enough to pass the child off as his."

"Tomas *is* his son!"

"I think you are lying," Diego said, shoving her to the ground, and then kicking her hard in the stomach.

Tomas let the comforter fall back down lower to the ground. He didn't understand what was happening, and he didn't want to watch anyone hurt his mamá. She said his father had a lot of dangerous enemies, and they'd gone over what he was to do several times if something like this were to happen. He was to stay under the bed and not make a sound. He could do that.

"Diego, please."

"You are nothing but a lying De La Vega whore."

"No, Diego!"

Tomas snuck another peek, and saw his mother lying on the floor, holding her arm out to the man as she pleaded with him. Diego ignored her, pointing something at her. Tomas let the comforter drop all the way to the floor.

"It's too late. You will die, and so will your bastard child when we find him."

"No!"

There was a loud crack, and then cruel laughter filled the air. "Say hi to my cousin in hell, bitch."

"You ready, Diego? The Don wants us back immediately. Something's happened."

"Yeah," Diego replied, laughing again. "We will hunt the kid down later."

"Are you going to kill him, too?" another voice asked.

"Depends," Diego said, as he walked toward the door. "We'll have a DNA test done. If he is Samuel's boy, we will raise him as a Valdez."

"And, if not?"

The voices were fading away, but Tomas distinctly heard Diego's response. "I will put a bullet between his eyes just like I did his mother."

Tomas laid on the floor in silence for a long time after they left, mindful of the fact that he was supposed to wait for his father to come for him. He wanted to go to his mother and check on her, as she hadn't moved since the men walked out, but he was afraid to. Finally, when he couldn't stand it anymore, he slowly slid out from under the bed and crawled over to his mother. The closer he got, the more he began to shake with fear. She was lying so still.

"Mamá," Tomas whispered, reaching out to touch her arm. She didn't move, didn't respond. "Mamá," he tried again, his voice cracking as several tears slipped free and trailed down his cheeks. His gaze went to her face, and he screamed, long and loud. She stared at him, her once beautiful, dark eyes wide open and vacant, a hole directly between them.

CHAPTER ONE

S alome let herself into the large, three-story home, sighing as she glanced at the thin, gold watch on her wrist. It was after midnight and she was drained. She just wanted to go upstairs, take a nice, long bubble bath, and then sleep for twenty-four solid hours. Unfortunately, that wasn't an option. First, she had to check in with her father —the controlling ass. She was twenty-eight years old, for fuck's sake. You'd think she would be able to make her own decisions by now. That's not the case when your father was Fabio Villanueva, owner of one of the largest restaurant franchises in Colombia. She worked for him, reported directly to him, and there were no exceptions. He demanded control over all things—including her.

Sighing, Salome slid her aching feet out of her four-inch-high heels. Picking them up, she walked down the long hall to her father's home office. He would hate that she was coming to him without her shoes, but she was beyond caring. Let him yell. It was all he seemed to do anymore, anyway; no matter how hard she tried to please him. She was just plain over it.

The thick, plush carpet muffled her steps, and she was at his door before she knew it. Taking a deep breath, she raised her hand to knock, but then froze when the sound of male voices drifted her way. One was her father's, the other one she didn't recognize, but it came over loud and clear through the speakerphone.

"Look, I know what I promised you, but if you will give me just a little more time…"

"You are out of time, Villanueva. You made a business proposition with my boss; one you didn't follow through with. You knew what the repercussions would be. As you were told in the beginning, if you can't come up with the money, we will collect it another way. We will be by within the hour to get the woman."

"Dammit, I need her."

"You should have thought of that before you made a deal with the devil."

"Salome isn't home yet," her father said, anger vibrating through his voice.

"Then we will wait," the tone was firm and unyielding. "See you soon, Fabio."

Her father swore loudly, and she heard a loud crash, as if he'd thrown the phone against the wall. "Son of a bitch!"

Salome stiffened, her eyes widening in shock as she slowly backed away from the door, her hand going to her mouth. Had she really just heard what she'd thought she heard? Did her father basically just *sell* her off to pay some kind of debt he owed? She swallowed hard, tears threatening to appear as she realized life as she knew it was about to drastically change, and not for the better. Someone would be there soon for her. And then what? The thoughts that flooded her mind terrified her.

Straightening her shoulders, she glared at the door. Fuck that! She wasn't going to sit around and wait to see who showed up. As much as she wanted to run in and confront the bastard, she knew she couldn't. She had to get out of there quickly.

"Now what, Father?"

Salome stifled the gasp that wanted to escape at the sound of her oldest brother's voice. Kain was a part of this? No, he couldn't be. He'd always protected her before. He wouldn't throw her to the wolves.

One tear slid free when she heard her baby brother, Giovanni, say, "We can't just hand Salome over to them, Papá."

"She's as good as dead if we do," Dario said gruffly.

They were all in there. Her entire family—deciding her fate.

"We don't have a choice," her father snapped. "We either give her to them, or we all die."

"I would rather die than hand my little sister over to some bastard who is going to hurt her," Kain growled. "What the fuck were you thinking making a deal like that, Father? We don't need the money that bad."

"It wasn't about the money."

"No," Dario interjected, "it was about you trying to climb higher in the organization."

Organization? What were they talking about? Salome moved cautiously back toward the office so she could hear better.

"Well, now it's about not getting a damn bullet between the eyes. We can either sit around here and whine and moan about it, or we can let them have Salome. I, for one, vote for the latter."

"It's not right, Papá," Gio shouted angrily. "She's our blood."

"Then you're a dead man," her father stated. "As are the rest of us."

"They won't kill her," Kain reasoned, suddenly changing his tune. "If we give her to them now, we can come up with a way to get her back."

What the hell? Was he seriously going to just hand her over to someone their own father feared?

"You're right, but how will she be when she comes home?" There was pain in Dario's voice, but he wasn't exactly protesting in her defense anymore.

"Broken," Gio cried. "She'll be broken, you assholes."

"Better she is broken than for all of us to be dead," Kain said raggedly. "Broken can be fixed, death cannot."

There it was. Her father, Kain, and Dario were voting to hand her over to whoever wanted her. Gio was the only one prepared to fight for her, but from the sounds of it, he would be no match against the Devil, whoever the hell that was.

Gritting her teeth, fighting against the agony searing her chest where her heart beat erratically, Salome turned silently and ran. Someone was coming for her, someone even her domineering tyrant of a father was afraid of, and she wasn't going to wait around for them.

Slipping up the stairs to her bedroom, Salome rushed over to her closet. It took her less than a minute to grab the wad of cash she had hidden in the back of it, and then she was gone again, not even taking time to pack a bag. She had to get out of there now before her family realized she was in the house.

Creeping back down the stairs, a lot slower than she'd gone up them, Salome made sure no one was around before leaving the house the same way she had come in. Soon, she was in her car, tossing her heels that she was still clutching tightly into the seat next to her. Starting the vehicle, she made her way down the long drive with her lights off and into the street, making sure she was a good half mile down the road before she turned them on.

She needed a plan. She wasn't going to get very far without one, especially in her own car. Someone would find her, whether it was her family, or whoever they were ready and willing to hand her over to. At this point, she wasn't sure which one would be worse. Her father might be an overbearing ass who dictated her life, but she never once doubted her brothers' love, not until tonight.

What was she going to do?

"Pull it together, Salome," she muttered, swiping at the tears that were now streaming down her face and blurring her vision. "You're stronger than this. Definitely stronger than those fuckers give you credit for." Slamming her fist against the steering wheel, she spat, "Do not let them win. Think dammit!"

Salome drove aimlessly for a good hour before her anguish began lifting enough for her to start devising a plan. She needed protection. She couldn't go to the police. Her father was in tight with several of the officers, not only the ones from the city they lived in but also the majority of the surrounding ones. She had no other family. No friends because Fabio Villanueva didn't believe his daughter needed any and had pushed away anyone who tried to get close to her. There was no one she trusted.

Frowning, Salome turned into the parking lot of a store that was open all night, where she could get something to change into. She was going to need clothes to wear that were different from her normal attire. An outfit more comfortable than the seven-hundred-dollar outfit she was currently sporting. Parking as close to the front door as possible, Salome slipped her feet into her shoes, then left the safety of her car to run inside so that she could pick up some necessities. Less than fifteen minutes later, she paid for her purchases and walked into the bathroom dressed in a power suit and her four-inch heels. She left in a pair of dark jeans, a gray graphic tee shirt covered by a black zip up hoodie, and black tennis shoes, the dress and heels now at the bottom of a trashcan.

Salome got back in her car, still mulling over where she could go for help, when a thought struck her. Instead of going to the police, what if she asked someone else for protection? Someone her father would never expect her to approach for help. Who better to go to when you couldn't seek help from the police than someone on the other side of the law?

The mafia.

She had heard rumors of the De La Vega Familia in Cali, one of the biggest crime syndicates in Colombia. There were whispers in the restaurants about them, both in awe and fear. But maybe, just maybe, they would help her. At least until she could figure out who was after her, besides her own family.

Once she found out who was a threat to her, she would go after the bastards herself, and rain down fire on them like they'd never seen before. They would see that Salome Villanueva was no wilting flower. She was powerful, determined to survive, and pissed the hell off.

CHAPTER TWO

K ain Villanueva held his anger in check, just barely. The rage that filled him at the thought of what his father was doing made it almost impossible not to pull his revolver out and put a bullet in the man's conniving heart. Salome was nothing like the rest of them. She had a heart of gold hidden beneath her tough, sassy exterior. She worked her ass off for their father and would do anything for Kain and their brothers. He loved her, dammit, whether he allowed himself to show it in front of everyone else or not. She was the one bright light in the Villanueva family. The one person, aside from Dario and Giovanni, that he trusted beyond a doubt. There was no way in hell the bastard who had his claws in their father would get his hands on her. Kain would die first.

"What are we going to do?" Dario whispered, his eyes on Fabio, who was pouring himself a shot of whiskey while they waited for the devil's minions to arrive.

"Whatever it takes," Kain muttered.

"Where the hell is Salome?" Fabio snapped, turning to glare at them. "She should have been home by now."

"Maybe she is?" Gio said, rising from his chair. "I'll go check."

"She's not here. She knows better than to go to her room without checking in with me first!"

Kain held up a hand with a short shake of his head to his brother. "I'll run up and see. They should be here anytime. It's been over an hour since their call." If he could get to her before they showed up, maybe he could get her out of the house through one of the hidden tunnels. Just one more thing in their lives that his little sister didn't know about. If she had any idea of the things they transported in and out through those tunnels, he was sure they would never hear the end of it.

The words had barely left his mouth when there was a thundering knock on the front door. Gio stiffened, his eyes darkening in anger as he glared at their father. "I can't fucking believe you are going to do this."

"Don't talk to me like that, boy!"

"Or what?" Gio sneered. "You'll sell me off to the highest bidder too?"

"I didn't sell Salome!"

"No," Dario cut in, "you just lost her in a gamble you should never had made."

Kain gritted his teeth, wishing he could tell his father how he really felt, too. But, as the eldest son, certain things were expected of him. Understanding, acceptance, loyalty. He would have to back the son of a bitch... for now.

When the knocking became louder and he knew their door was about to be kicked in, Kain motioned to Gio. "Go. Run up and see if Salome is in her room." While he preferred to go himself, Fabio would frown upon him leaving the confrontation that was about to take place. When Gio turned his glare on him, Kain returned it with one of his own.

"Now, Gio!" their father roared, stalking past them to walk to the front of the house.

Kain grabbed Gio's arm when he went to follow. "I'm with Father. I doubt she's up there. She never misses a nightly check in."

"And if she is?" Gio demanded angrily, lifting his eyebrows in question.

"Show her the tunnel that will take her to the furthest point of our property. I don't give a fuck what the old man says. Salome is our sister. Familia. We are not handing her over to be used and abused by anyone, least of all the likes of that bastard he is in so deep with."

Gio's jaw hardened, and he gave a quick nod before leaving the room.

"I hate that fucking prick," Dario snarled. "If it were up to me, he would already be six feet under. What kind of man gives his own daughter to the enemy knowing damn well what's going to happen to her?"

"The kind that doesn't deserve to live," Kain muttered. "But, for now, we play the game and do whatever needs to be done to keep Salome safe."

"Agreed."

Kain heard voices as he made his way down the long hall to the front door. Glancing up, he saw the back of his brother as he reached the top of the stairs and turned left toward Salome's room. Gio would keep her safe if she was home, of that Kain had no doubt. He might be young, only twenty-five years old, but the man was as deadly as they came.

"Where is the woman? It isn't a good idea to keep the boss waiting."

"You kept us waiting," Fabio said, arching an eyebrow at them.

Kain kept his mouth shut. It wasn't a good idea to aggravate the men in front of him, not if you wanted to live. Apparently, his father had forgotten that.

The man on the right took a step forward, pulling a gun from a holster at his hip and placing the barrel to Fabio's forehead, all in one smooth motion. "You were asked a question. We will not ask again."

"She's not here." Kain glanced up at Gio as he descended the stairs, his brow furrowed in a small frown. "She's not answering her cell phone, and there isn't anyone at the restaurant."

The man pulled the gun from Fabio and pointed it at Gio. "Did someone tip the bitch off that we were coming for her?"

Gio stiffened, his face becoming a dark mask. Before he could reply, Kain stepped between the two of them. "We've all been with our father since the phone call took place. No one contacted Salome. I have no idea where she is, but we will find out." And then they would hide her from all of this, just like they had ever since she was born. No matter how strong his sister was, this was not the life for her. There was too much death and destruction. She deserved better.

The gun in the other man's hand that was now pointed at Kain's chest, didn't waiver as he growled, "You better

17

find her. You have twenty-four hours. After that, we will come for you. One by one."

"Understood."

"The boss isn't going to be happy," the first man said, shaking his head. "He's going to be pissed, so I suggest you hurry." Ignoring Fabio, he handed a card over to Kain. "Call me when you find her."

"I'm the Don of this household," Fabio stated, narrowing his eyes on the men, "not Kain."

"You sure as fuck don't act like it," the second man said, holstering his gun and turning to leave without a backward glance.

Kain watched them go, aware of his father swearing loudly and stalking away back toward his office. Once everyone was gone, he looked over at Gio and demanded, "What aren't you telling us?"

Gio seemed to hesitate before he moved closer to him and Dario. "She was here."

Kain froze, contemplating what his little brother was telling him. "How do you know?"

"Her closet door was open, and there were some clothes on the floor, like they'd fallen off the hangers."

Kain frowned. "Salome is meticulous about her wardrobe. There's no way she would have knocked them off the hangers and left them there."

"There's more." Gio glanced over his shoulder, making sure they were alone before he whispered, "She had some money hidden in the back of her closet. It's gone. All of it."

"How much are we talking?" Dario demanded. "And, how the hell do you know she had it hidden there?"

Gio swallowed hard, letting his head drop before he

replied, "She showed me one time. Told me it was there in case I ever needed to get away."

"Get away?"

"From him."

Kain didn't need him to clarify who Gio meant. They all knew. Fabio Villanueva was not a nice man. If he was angry, they all felt his wrath. No one was excluded.

"How much?" Dario asked again.

"Last time I knew, it was close to a grand. It may be more now, but not much. It won't get her far."

"Shit," Kain growled, raking a hand through his hair. "We need to find her."

"Do you think she overheard us?"

Gio's quiet question was one that had been running through Kain's mind ever since he found out Salome was gone. "Yeah," he muttered, "she heard. I'm sure of it."

"So, our sister is out there, all alone, thinking none of us love her enough to protect her," Dario said gruffly. "Which couldn't be further from the truth."

"Yeah."

"Dammit, we didn't mean the things we said. We just needed time to figure shit out."

"True, but she doesn't know that." Kain sighed, feeling as if the weight of the world was on his shoulders. He was the oldest. It was his job to protect his siblings, and he was doing a shitty job of it.

"We have to find her," Gio rasped, his hands clenched tightly at his sides. "She's going to get herself killed."

"That's where you're wrong, Little Brother." When Gio met his gaze, Kain ground out, "If anything happens to Salome, it falls directly on my shoulders."

"Ours," Dario corrected. "She is ours to protect."

"One thing worries me," Gio said, glancing back down the long hallway again before bringing his eyes back to them. "They aren't going to stand down, are they?"

"Not a chance." Kain knew they wouldn't, because if it were him, there was no way he would.

"They gave us twenty-four hours to find her."

"Yes, Gio, but they will be looking for her, too."

"Fuck."

"The race is on," Dario said, his hand going to the Glock that rested on his hip. "I, for one, refuse to lose. I will do whatever it takes to find Salome and keep her safe."

"Familia first," Kain said, nodding to his brothers.

"Familia first," they replied in unison, raising their fists and bumping them to his.

CHAPTER THREE

Tomas glared down at the man who was cowering before him, not feeling the least bit sympathetic. He'd heard the same whiny spiel from the drug dealer for the past three months. What the bastard didn't realize was that Tomas and his brothers had looked into his story, so deep they'd turned up more shit than even Tomas wanted to think about. He was a liar, a cheat, and a murderer of young women and children. Tomas would kill him for that alone.

"Shut the fuck up, Cortes," he snarled, slamming a boot into the side of the guy's head. "I don't want to hear your bullshit anymore. We know you've been stealing money from us, and we know what you've been spending it on."

"No! I would never…"

"I think this son of a bitch needs a lesson in what happens to someone who has the balls to lie to a De La Vega, Brother," Mateo said, slowly walking in a circle around the man. It was dark, the only light came from streetlamps on either end of the alley, and a dimly lit bulb above a door behind them.

"Idiot." Javier walked over to lean against a brick wall, crossing his arms over his thick chest as he glared down at Orlando Cortes. They were in an alley located behind a building owned by the De La Vega family, where their cocaine was made and Cortes distributed for them. He was one of the many dealers they had throughout the country and in the United States. One they wouldn't miss if he was gone. There were several more waiting in line to take his place. The De La Vega family ran a huge business and were known for paying their employees well.

"Look, it wasn't me!"

"Lies," Tomas grunted, slamming his fist into the side of Orlando's head, dropping him all the way to the ground. "We've been tracking you and your financials for months now. We know exactly how much you have taken. Not only that, but we know what you've been spending our money on."

"We know," Mateo cut in, "and we do not approve of it, you sick fucker."

"You will die," Javier stated, nodding in Tomas' direction. "And my brother will not make it easy on you."

Orlando lay with his cheek against the hard concrete, staring up at Tomas, his eyes wide with fear. It was obvious he'd heard of Tomas and how he liked to play with his victims, especially scum like himself. "I'll pay it back," he rasped as he slowly pushed himself up on shaking arms. "All of it! I swear!"

"Where are you going to find five hundred thousand dollars?" Mateo asked, cocking an eyebrow.

"Five hundred thousand?" Orlando squeaked, slowly

rising to his feet, swaying back and forth as he stared at them in terror. "That's more than double the amount…"

"The Don requires interest paid on all loans."

"You are forgetting something, Mateo," Tomas said, sliding a Glock from the holster at his back.

"What's that, Brother?"

"The Don didn't loan this bastard a dime." Tomas pointed the gun at the sniveling man and pulled the trigger. Orlando screamed when his kneecap shattered, falling to the ground again. Tears streamed down the dealer's face as he begged for his life, but Tomas wasn't moved. It was his job to take care of slime like this, and a part of him enjoyed it. He didn't enjoy the actual killing itself, but more in causing pain and suffering to those who had wronged his family and got sick pleasure out of hurting the innocent. Tomas may take lives, but never the life of an innocent person. No, the scum he killed definitely deserved a bullet in the head.

"You fucking broke my leg!" Orlando cried, rocking back and forth as he clutched at his thigh, right above the bloody mess that was left of his knee.

A slow, wicked grin curved Tomas' lip. Taking aim, he pulled the trigger again, watching in satisfaction as dark red blood began to seep from the hole he just put in Orlando's hand.

"Fuck!" Orlando's screams echoed throughout the alley, but Tomas wasn't worried they would be heard. It was almost three in the morning, and no one was around except for the piece of shit who was lying on the ground in front of him, fresh piss staining his crotch.

"There are three things in this world that our father cannot stand," Mateo stated, crouching down next to the man. "Being lied to, stolen from, and made a fool of. You have lied frequently to, not only your superiors, but even directly to my brother, Javier, several times in the past few months. You have stolen an exorbitant amount of money from my familia."

Tomas put his Glock back in its holster and then removed a knife from the sheath in his boot. Stalking over to Orlando, he grabbed what was left of the man's hair and yanked his head back, placing the blade to his throat.

"The only thing you have not done so far is make a fool of Don De La Vega," Mateo growled. "I will not allow it."

One nod from his brother was all it took, and Tomas slid the blade deep into Orlando's skin across his throat, ending his miserable excuse of a life.

"Let's clean up this mess and go home," Mateo said, sighing heavily as he rose, brushing off his dark slacks. "It's late."

"I got it," Tomas told him, wiping the blade of his knife on Orlando's filthy jeans before putting it back in his boot. He would clean it better when he got home, but this would have to do for now. "Go home. You have a meeting with Father at the ass crack of dawn."

"So do you," Javier drawled, shoving off of the brick wall and sauntering over toward them.

Tomas shrugged. "I don't sleep."

"Maybe you should try it sometime," Mateo suggested dryly. "Might help your disposition."

"Might help yours if you got laid," Javier shot back, more as a teasing dig at Mateo than in defense of Tomas. He paused, a slow mischievous grin appearing. "Although, I could say that about both of you."

Tomas flipped him off, then turned to make his way down the alley.

"Hey, where the hell are you going?" Mateo called out. "I thought you were taking care of this?"

Glancing back, Tomas raised an eyebrow. "To get my car. You want to lug his huge ass all the way down the alley?"

Mateo's gaze went from Orlando to Tomas, then back to Orlando as he slowly shook his head. "Naw, man. You got this."

"I always do," Tomas muttered, shaking his head at the thought of his brothers doing the dirty work he did. Not that they hadn't killed before. Both had taken lives, just not to the extent Tomas had. He was their cleanup man. It's what he did. What he was good at. What he preferred. Eldest son or not, he had no desire to lead, even if he could have. He would leave that shit to Mateo.

CHAPTER FOUR

The sun was just coming up when Salome pulled into the parking lot of a gas station on the outskirts of Cali. She was utterly exhausted, but her car was on empty and she needed some caffeine. What she really wanted was sleep, but that wasn't going to happen anytime soon. Not until she managed to track down the De La Vega family and beg them for protection. One way or another, she would get some rest after that.

Not for the first time, Salome was second guessing her rash decision to go to the mafia for help. She wasn't stupid. She knew this could go a few different ways. She just prayed it was the way she was hoping for and not one of the other alternatives... being turned away, finding herself a prisoner and placed in the same predicament she was currently in with the man she only knew as the "Devil", or possibly worse—a permanent dirt nap.

Sighing, Salome got out of the vehicle that had been running on fumes for the past couple of miles and made her way inside. She needed help, and there was no one else. She would be placing her life in the hands of Don De La Vega, but she had no other choice. Her death was imminent otherwise, because she refused to bow down to the man threatening her family. She was no coward.

Moving quickly once she entered the gas station, Salome used the restroom and then grabbed something to eat and a coffee. She wasn't sure she would be able to stomach the food, but she knew she needed something in her system to keep going. She was just getting ready to go to the front and pay when the bell on the door jingled, indicating there was a new customer. She glanced over and froze.

A police officer entered, and the way he was casing the area, it was obvious they were looking for someone. Salome's eyes went to the window and her heart began to race when she saw the police car parked behind her own, lights flashing. Shit! Somehow, they'd found her already. She'd known her father had ties in the police department but hadn't realized they reached this far.

Or did they? She was only a few hours away from home.

Salome frowned, making sure to stay halfway hidden in one of the aisles behind a row of candy as she watched the policeman walk over to the register and hand the clerk a picture. "Have you seen this woman?"

The man's eyes widened slightly, and he slowly shook his head. "No, Sir, I haven't seen her."

"Are you sure?"

"I'd remember someone that looked like that," the clerk replied, his eyes still on the picture.

Salome ducked her head; glad she'd shoved her hair up in a ponytail in the hood of her sweatshirt. The long mass of thick, dark hair with streaks of ruby red throughout would definitely attract attention. It always did, which was why her father insisted she put the damn things in every few months. The first time she'd tried adding the fiery red color had been on a whim. She'd needed a change in her life, and if she were honest, at the time she'd been in a sour mood and was hoping it would piss her father off. But what she realized instead was that she was turning heads of men she had no desire to get to know, causing more interest and sideways glances at the restaurants when she was working, and it made her feel more than a little uncomfortable. She'd wanted to remove them, but her father wouldn't allow it. He liked them, so they stayed.

The bells on the door jingled again as another policeman walked in. "It's her car, but there's no sign of her outside."

Salome cringed, fighting the urge to run for the door. That confirmed what she'd already known, even if she wanted to deny it. She was the woman they were looking for. How the hell had they found her so quickly?

Her father must have contacted them as soon as he figured out she was missing. Unless… maybe it wasn't her father after all. Maybe it was the person he'd been planning on handing her over to. He had to be a powerful man, whoever the hell he was, to make Fabio Villanueva fear him.

With that thought came guilt. If he was that powerful, what would he do to her brothers when he found out she'd ran? She was angry at them for siding with their father, hurt that they would even consider sending her away with someone others thought of as the Devil, but she didn't want them dead. She loved them, even after what she heard just hours ago.

Salome slowly sat her coffee down on the counter next to her, along with the food, and began to back away toward the door she'd seen in the rear of the building by the restrooms. It didn't matter how much she loved them; she wasn't going to willingly walk into hell after they all sold her down the river, not unless it was a hell of her own choosing. No. She would figure out a way out of this mess that would keep them all alive.

"Check the bathrooms."

Those were the last words she heard as she slipped out the back door and into the early morning light, finding herself in an alley. Wasting no time, Salome ran down the short strip of gravel heading to a street that led into a small housing district. A small shiver of dread ran down her spine as she glanced around at the seedier looking homes. It was a rundown area, where some homes seemed abandoned while others had broken windows or windows that were boarded up, but still showed signs of life in them.

No one appeared to be outside, but Salome swore she could feel eyes on her, watching her, stalking her. A soft cry of fear escaping, she cut through another alley behind a garage, coming out onto a sidewalk at the end and kept going at a fast pace until she was a good five blocks away, before turning down another street that she assumed would take her further into the city.

She walked with her hands shoved into the pockets of her sweatshirt, her shoulders hunched as she tried to appear as nonchalant as possible at the ass crack of dawn, making her way through Cali, wishing she would have thought to bring a weapon with her. She'd been around guns all her life, even had a small derringer she normally shoved into her purse if she went any place where she worried about her safety. It wouldn't kill anyone, but it would sure as hell stop them in their tracks so she could get away if she were threatened. Why hadn't she thought to bring it with her? Probably because all she could think about at the time was running for her damn life. She didn't even have her purse, which meant she had no ID on her. She'd forgotten the damn thing at work again. A normal occurrence after a fifteen-hour shift. Pushing the thought aside, she gritted her teeth and quickened her pace.

Twenty minutes later Salome finally breathed a sigh of relief when she found herself in a busier part of the city that seemed to be slowly waking up. More people were out, probably on their way to work, and she was able to merge with them to help hide her presence from anyone who might be out looking for her.

The problem was that eventually someone, whether it be her family or the man her father owed money to, would catch up with her. They had already found her car. They knew where she was, and while Cali was a huge city, she wasn't going to be able to hide in it forever. Her only chance at surviving the fucked-up mess she found herself in was the De La Vega family, but she had no idea how to find them.

There was a loud honk a few feet away, and then yelling, and another honk. Salome glanced over in that direction, careful to keep the side of her face hidden as much as possible in her hood, and her breath caught in her throat as her gaze landed on a taxi. An idea began to form, and before she could talk herself out of it, she sprinted down to the end of the block and pounded on the passenger side window to get the driver's attention. He rolled down the window, glaring at her. "What do you want, lady?"

"I need a ride," she rasped, before opening the back door and slipping inside the car. Her feet were killing her, and she let out a small groan as she leaned back against the seat. Her entire body ached right now, and her breath was coming out in small pants after her hike through the city.

The man's eyes narrowed on her as he took in her disheveled appearance, then he shook his head. "You have to pay."

"I will."

Giving her a calculating stare, he cocked his head to the side, ignoring the horns that were now blaring around them as he sat idling at the stop sign at the busy intersection. "Where do you want to go, lady?"

Salome's hands trembled slightly as she reached into her jean pocket and pulled out a handful of bills. Selecting a few, she handed them to him. "I will give you this much now, and the rest when we get there."

He slowly counted out the money he held, his eyes widening, before a deep frown appeared. "Where am I taking you?"

Taking a calculated risk, figuring that the majority of the people in the city would know where the mafia leader would live, she lifted her chin, squared her shoulders, and met his eyes. "To the De La Vega Familia."

The man slowly shook his head and tried to hand the

money back to her. "No, lady. That is no place for someone like you."

"That is the *only* place for me right now," Salome said quietly, suddenly certain she was right.

He stared at her in silence for a moment, and then slowly turned around and put the car in gear. "Doesn't matter to me none. You pay, I take you."

CHAPTER FIVE

"It's been taken care of, yes, Mateo?" It was more of a statement than a question. The Don knew if he gave an order to his sons, they would follow through.

"Yes, Father, it is done," Mateo replied smoothly, shouldering most of the conversation in their early morning meeting as their father's second.

"The body?"

"Tomas disposed of it."

Miguel grunted his approval. They all knew if Tomas got rid of someone, they would never be found. Mateo and Javier had asked him a few times what he did with the bodies, but he shrugged them off. He didn't necessarily care for the part of his job that had him out digging holes in the middle of the night in a fucking forest, but he tried to protect his brothers from it as much as possible. The less they knew, the better. "Good. Who did you move up to take his place?"

"Raul Reyes. Things should run much more smoothly now."

Raul had been on their payroll for the past six years. He did what he was told, worked hard, and was extremely loyal. He had proven himself, and they all trusted him, however, that didn't mean they weren't going to keep a close eye on him as he stepped into his new position in their organization. They'd trusted Orlando too until the bastard got greedy.

"I agree. He will do fine. He's a good man."

Tomas stood by the window, his back to his family as he stared out over the large expanse of lawn in front of him. They lived in a large villa on a hill, surrounded by trees. The closest home to theirs was a good five miles down the road, and that was the way they liked it. There was a tall, wrought-iron fence surrounding the area, and no less than five guards patrolling the boundary lines both day and night. There were also cameras located in various places throughout the villa, and a person manning them at all times. With the kind of business they ran, there could never be a thing as too much protection.

Rubbing a hand over his face, Tomas smothered a yawn. He was tired. He hadn't made it home until just a couple of hours ago, which had given him just enough time to shower, clean his weapons, and take a quick twenty-minute catnap before the meeting.

"What about the shipment we sent to the US?"

Tomas turned from the window, leaning back against the wall and crossing his arms over his chest. He needed to pay attention to the conversation, even if he had no desire to be involved in it. Give him action over this shit any day.

"It made it there with no complications and is already being distributed along the east coast," Mateo replied. "I would like to suggest expanding to the west coast. California, Arizona, and Nevada specifically."

"You have contacts there?"

"No," Mateo admitted, "but Javier does."

"Is that so?" Miguel questioned, raising an eyebrow as he looked at his youngest son. "I wasn't aware that you knew anyone in the United States."

Javier shrugged, "I've met a few online." When their father's eyebrow rose even higher, he said, "Don't worry, I've been looking closely into all the ones I would even consider approaching about something like this, along with their immediate and extended families. I've already eliminated the ones with any connections to law enforcement or that I don't think would be a good fit. With your approval, I will be taking a more in depth look at the others in the next couple of weeks."

"You and your damn hacking abilities," Mateo muttered, shaking his head as he shot a grin at his brother. "I swear, you spend more time on a computer than anything else. Which one of us needs to get laid?"

"Probably all of you," Miguel said dryly. "Your Mamá has been looking for grandchildren for the past couple of years now." Raising a hand to hold off any responses, he went on, "Dig deeper into their lives, Javier. While I do agree expansion into the west coast could be beneficial, as long as we can keep up with the supply and demand, we can't afford to approach the wrong person with something like this."

"Agreed."

"Take your time on this. Bring what you come up with next month and we will discuss it again. Mateo, I want you to..." before he could go on, there was a knock on the door. Miguel frowned at the interruption as everyone in the villa knew they were not to be disturbed while in a closed-door meeting. "Enter!"

A smile appeared when the door opened and his wife, Sofia, walked into the room. She was the only one who was exempt when it came to certain rules of the house. Mateo's and Javier's mother was petite, with thick black hair showing hints of gray, falling just past her shoulders. She had soft hazel eyes that could turn hard in an instant if you threatened her family, and the gentlest soul and kindest heart. She took Tomas in and raised him as her own after the death of his birth mother. She loved him, even knowing he came from Miguel's mistress—a woman she found out about the night his father brought him home, when there was nowhere else for him to go. Not once had she treated him differently, even after Mateo and Javier were born.

"I'm sorry to interrupt, but there appears to be a small disturbance at the front gate, Miguel."

His father and brothers stood in unison, the same time Tomas pushed away from the wall, ready to confront the threat. Sofia shook her head, holding up a hand as she blocked the doorway. "No, it's not what you think. From what the guards say, it is a young woman asking for our help. She's in trouble, and you need to hear her out."

Miguel sighed, crossing the room to pull his wife into his arms. "Sofia, you have such a tender heart, but you need to let us do this our way. She could be an enemy."

"You don't know that."

"You don't know she isn't, Love."

His father was right, but Tomas could tell Sofia wasn't backing down either. For some reason, she'd already decided the woman was innocent, and it was going to take a lot to convince her otherwise.

"I saw her on the screens, Miguel. I watched her for a long time before coming to you. She's trying to act strong, but I see the terror in her eyes. I don't think she wants to be here. I believe she had no choice."

Miguel placed a gentle kiss on her forehead, before promising, "We will listen to her first, and find out exactly what is going on before we make any decisions."

"I'm going with you."

"No, Sofia."

"Yes, I am," Sofia insisted, pulling away from Miguel and glaring at him. "That young woman is going to need someone in her corner from the beginning, and it sure as hell doesn't look like it will be any of you."

"Now, Mamá," Mateo said soothingly, "you know we always treat women with the respect due to them."

Which was Mateo's way of saying, if the woman really was innocent, they would extend their protection to her. If she wasn't, she would die, plain and simple.

When Sofia narrowed her eyes on Mateo, and he could see the anger lurking in the depths of them, Tomas stepped in. "I will handle it, Mamá. If she needs our protection, and is not a threat to the family, I will keep her safe from whatever it is she is running from."

A wide smile spread across Sofia's face and she gave him a nod. "That's a good boy, Tomas. I can always count on you. Now, let's go." Turning, she stalked out of the room, not waiting to see if they followed. It was obvious she was intent on going with them, no matter what they thought.

When Mateo started to argue against their mother

being a part of whatever was about to take place, Miguel shook his head. "You know when your mother gets in one of her moods, there is no swaying her. You will learn someday that there is a time to stand your ground, but there is also a time to give in, so your woman is happy. Now, let's go get this done with."

Tomas followed his father and brothers out into the hallway and down the stairs, laughing inwardly. Sofia was a kind, sweet person who always tried to do whatever she could for others, but she also had a spine of steel. If someone came after her family, she would not hesitate to retaliate. Even his own father wasn't exempt from her wrath. After she found out about his mistress years ago, Miguel never had another. Tomas had heard a rumor about a knife near his father's balls, but he'd never actually gotten the full story, so he wasn't sure if it was true or not.

Tomas, Mateo, and Javier dropped just one step behind their parents as they left the house to walk down to the gate. As much as Tomas would prefer to be in front of them in case things went to shit, he was showing deference to his parents by letting them lead, as were Mateo and Javier... for now. If the woman proved to be an enemy, he and his brothers would take over while Miguel got their mother the hell out of there.

Tomas took in the scene, sudden anger filled him at the sight of a figure kneeling on the ground, arms wrapped tightly around their waist, their bowed head covered by a hood. Even from a distance, he could tell she was terrified. But why the fuck was she on the ground? Had someone hurt the woman already without giving them a chance to speak to her? Nothing pissed him off more than violence toward a woman.

"What's going on here?" Miguel demanded as soon as they reached their guards. When no one responded, he growled, "I have asked you a question. I will not ask again."

"Eh, she got a little feisty," Martin said with a shrug and a grin. "I just gave her a couple of smacks and a nudge to the ground."

"You hit her?" Sofia gasped, taking a step toward the woman before Javier grabbed her and held her back.

"Mamá, wait. Let us talk to her first."

Tomas moved around his parents and walked over to the woman. She was so small, her shoulders shaking as she huddled on the ground in front of him. Ignoring everything else, he crouched down in front of her, placing a finger under her chin. Gently, he tilted her face up to meet his, rage punching him in the gut at the sight of the blood marring her lips and the discoloration that had already started around her right eye.

"Tomas…"

He heard the warning tone in Mateo's voice, but it was too late. He was on his feet, across the distance that separated him from the son of a bitch who had done this to her, his fist slamming into the fucker's face. "You think it's funny to beat on a woman?" he snarled, letting another fist fly, this time connecting with Martin's gut and putting the man on his knees. "You make her bleed; I make you bleed." One more punch was all it took. There was a satisfying crunch as the man's nose was busted and blood spurted out around them.

"Tomas, please, you don't want to scare her any more than she already is."

Sofia's voice managed to penetrate his wall of rage,

just as he was lifting his arm again, stopping him from landing a deadly blow.

"He isn't scaring me."

Tomas took a step back, wiping his bloody fist on his jeans, before turning to face the others. His eyes connected with wild, angry, dark green ones. There was a hint of fear in them, but it didn't seem to be directed toward him.

"Sorry," he said gruffly, well aware that he never apologized for anything to anyone, except maybe to Sofia. He heard his mother's soft gasp of surprise, but ignored it, focusing on the woman in front of him.

"Don't be," she whispered. A single lone tear escaped, making its way down her cheek. Slowly, she reached up and removed her hood, revealing black hair with red throughout it, pulled back away from her face. She was stunning, even with the bruising on her delicate skin. "I appreciate what you did for me. Thank you."

Tomas knew he should be asking her questions, putting her through an inquisition, but all he could think about was what that mass of dark hair would look like if he took it down. What it would feel like if he ran his hands through it.

"My son has never condoned anyone hurting women," Sofia said, giving her a gentle smile. "To be honest, Martin is lucky he is still alive."

Tomas stiffened, glancing over at Sofia before looking back to the woman. What the hell did his mother think she was doing, telling a stranger something like that? Even if it was the truth.

The woman's eyes grew rounder, but then they narrowed on Martin, who was trying to struggle to his feet. "That asshole is just lucky my brothers aren't here. If they were…" she stopped, her pretty eyes clouding over as she lowered her head. "At least, in the past they would have done the same thing," it came out as a whisper, so soft Tomas had to strain to hear it.

"Maybe we should take this inside," Mateo suggested, his eyes roving over the area as if expecting an ambush.

"Agreed, Mateo," Miguel said, turning back toward the house. "We will meet in the family room. Javier, let's get your mother back in the house."

Tomas knew they were right. If this was some kind of ploy to get to their family, which he was highly doubting at this point that it was, they were all vulnerable out in the open. *But, should they just invite her into their home like that, not having a clue who she was?*

"Come on, Mamá." Javier slipped an arm around Sofia's waist and began to coax her toward the house. "Let's get out of the open."

"Tomas, remember your promise," Sofia said, before allowing her son to draw her away from them.

"What promise?" the woman asked, looking up at him with those big, emerald-colored eyes.

Mateo laughed, clapping Tomas on the shoulder. "My big brother here has taken on the role of your protector," he said in a teasing tone, but then that tone turned deadly. "Unless, of course, you are out to hurt our family. Then, he will be your executioner."

She nodded slowly, her eyes never leaving Tomas'. She seemed to ignore the last part of the statement, focusing on the first part instead. "That sounds good. I could use a protector right now."

Ignoring his brother, Tomas lifted his hand and gently

wiped away another tear that appeared. "What's your name?"

Her eyes drifted shut for a moment, and she seemed to lean into his touch, before she whispered, "Salome. Salome Villanueva."

"Well, fuck," Mateo grunted, moving past them. "A Villanueva within our walls. This ought to go over well."

CHAPTER SIX

S alome cringed at the man's words. They had heard of the Villanueva name, and it didn't sound like they were very thrilled about it. Could she be lucky enough that maybe it was a *different* Villanueva family and not her own that they seemed to despise? With the way her luck had been going, the answer was probably no.

Salome followed the tall, stocky man into the house, aware of the much more silent presence behind her. Tomas, they'd called him. He'd been her knight in shining armor after that asshole had hit her. She'd taken hits in the past from her father when he struck out in anger, but nothing like what she'd just gone through. And never from someone she didn't know, who was intent on hurting her. He'd even laughed when she fell to the ground after one of his fists connected with her ribs. It hurt like a bitch, and she raised a hand to cover the throbbing pain.

"What's wrong?"

His voice was low and gruff, and so fucking sexy. Just

like the man himself with his piercing, intense eyes and bad boy vibe he gave off.

"Nothing."

Tomas stopped her with a hand on her arm in the large entryway of the house. Glancing back at him, she cocked an eyebrow in question.

"Don't start this relationship off with lies, me and my family won't tolerate it. My father will be able to tell, and it won't end well for you."

Her brow furrowed in confusion as she met his dark gaze. "What do you mean?"

"You just lied to me, Salome. I asked you what was wrong. I expect an answer."

"Oh," Salome whispered, slowly dropping her hand away from her ribs.

"Tomas, are you coming?"

His eyes didn't leave hers as he hollered back, "We'll be there in a minute."

He wasn't giving in, she realized. If she didn't respond, she could kiss their help goodbye. And while she was shaking with nerves right now, she was hopeful they would extend their protection to her. Sighing, she slowly lifted her shirt up just enough to display the light bruising that was already beginning to show on her ribs. "My face wasn't the only thing he hit."

Tomas reached out as if to touch her skin, but hesitated before letting his hand fall back to his side. "I'm going to fucking kill him."

"Can it wait until after the meeting?" the one they called Mateo asked dryly as he appeared in the entryway. "Mamá is getting antsy."

Salome didn't move as she waited for Tomas to reply.

She didn't think he would really kill the guard… would he? Hell, he was in the mafia, but he didn't know her. Why would he kill for her?

"Yeah, but let's get this over with."

Salome slowly let her shirt fall back down and then turned to follow Mateo with Tomas right behind her. They went down a hall on the main level and entered a large room with a television on one wall, a couch facing it, and two more on each side. Sofia was already seated in the middle of one of them. Her other son sat next to her while her husband stood behind them, facing the door as if waiting for them to walk through it so he could decide her fate.

Which was exactly what he was doing, Salome realized, flinching when she saw the butt of a gun inside his suit coat. His hard gaze followed her as she walked over and sat down stiffly on the couch across from Sofia. To her surprise, Tomas sat beside her, leaning forward, his forearms on his thighs. She shuddered when she saw the outline of a gun at the small of his back, and for the first time she wondered if they were all carrying? It would make sense but hadn't been something that crossed her mind the entire time she was making her way to them for help.

"Her name is Salome Villanueva," Mateo said casually, as he made his way to the other couch.

"You have got to be kidding me," Javier muttered, glaring in her direction. "You let a fucking Villanueva in our house, brother?"

"A name does not make a person, Javier," Sofia cut in gently, patting her son's knee. "How about we let Salome tell us her story before passing judgment?"

When no one else interjected, Salome took a deep breath. "As Mateo said, my name is Salome. My father is Fabio Villanueva." When Javier swore loudly, her fears from before were confirmed. It was her family they didn't like for some reason. "I can tell his name means something to you, but I honestly don't know why. I'm assuming it has nothing to do with the restaurants he owns?"

"You have no idea what your father and brothers do?" Mateo asked her, and she could hear the suspicion in his voice.

"Well, no, not really. I help with the restaurants. I float back and forth between them, making sure everything runs smoothly." She did a hell of a lot more than just help out, but she wasn't going to get into that right now.

"You seriously come from a family like theirs and have no idea what the hell they do?" Javier asked incredulously. Shaking his head, he looked over at Tomas. "I'm sorry, man, but she's got to be fucking lying."

Tomas moved so fast; Salome cried out in fear before she could stop herself. One moment he was casually sitting there, listening to the conversation. The next, he had an arm around her, holding her snuggly against him. A hand was wrapped around her hair, pulling it just enough to cause a bite of pain as he held her still. She fought back tears, not wanting to appear weak in front of them. Clenching her jaw tightly, she brought one hand up to rest against his chest, but didn't push him away. Her fingers rested on something beneath his shirt, and she realized it was a cross. For some reason, that gave her hope.

"I'm not lying," she gasped, her eyes meeting his. "I don't have a clue what you all are talking about."

"Why are you here?" he demanded, his hand tightening in her hair.

"Because, I need your help. I…" Salome let her eyes close for a second, before once again opening them to meet his. "I don't know where else to go."

The tears she'd been struggling to hold in for so long burst forth and began streaming down her face. There wasn't anything she could do to stop it, as she whispered, "I came home last night after work to hear my father on the phone. It appears he owes someone money and can't pay up. So, they said they were coming for me."

"What?" Sofia gasped. "Surely he said they couldn't have you?"

Salome's eyes never left the man's in front of her, as she admitted, "It was a deal he made with them. If he couldn't pay, the man could have me. My brothers…" her voice broke, and it was a moment before she could continue. "They were all in his office with him. They didn't want to let whoever was on the phone take me, but Father said it would be better to hand me over than have them all be killed. That they could get me back someday."

"Kain didn't agree to that, did he?" Tomas growled, his deep brown eyes darkening even more.

"Not at first, but then he and Dario seemed to cave. Not Giovanni, though." A harsh laugh left her, as she rasped, "Gio is the only one who would have fought for me. I couldn't let him die for me."

"Even though they were ready to hand you over to someone where your fate could have been worse?"

Salome's chin trembled as she cried, "They are my family!"

47

"Who is this man who is after you?" Miguel asked, coming from behind the couch to sit next to his wife.

"I don't know," Salome admitted. "But whoever was on the phone told my father he shouldn't have made a deal with the Devil. So, that's what I've been calling him in my head."

"Why did you come here instead of going to the police?" Javier asked, and she could still hear the suspicion in his voice.

"Because, my father has ties with the police in our city. I just didn't realize it stretched this far."

"What do you mean?"

"They found my car at a gas station on the edge of town. I was inside the building getting food and something to drink when they showed up. They came inside looking for me."

The hold on her hair slowly loosened. "You're sure it was you they were looking for?"

Salome nodded, wincing at the pain in her head. Not so much where he still held her, but from the headache that had begun forming after that asshole, Martin, had hit her. "Yes."

"What did you do?"

"The only thing I could do," Salome whispered. "I ran."

CHAPTER SEVEN

Tomas stared at the woman in front of him, who bravely returned his look. He could tell she was in pain but didn't once complain about the way he was holding her. Suddenly, her eyes widened in horror and she gasped, "Oh no! I am so sorry!"

"For what," he asked, arching an eyebrow.

"What if I led the police here? To your door?" For the first time since he grabbed her, she tried to pull away. "I need to go!"

"Salome," he interrupted, trying not to laugh. "You aren't making any sense."

Glaring at him, she let out a small huff. "Yes, I am, you just aren't listening to me."

"Did you come to us for help, sweetheart?"

"Yes, but…"

"Do you know who we are? What we do?"

Her cheeks darkened a pretty pink, and she squeezed her eyes shut tight. "You're the mafia."

So she did know.

"And, just how do you know that?" Javier demanded.

Tomas shot a warning glare at his little brother, needing him to shut the hell up so he could get to the bottom of what was happening right now.

"I've heard the De La Vega name in our restaurants before. I don't know much about the mafia, but with my father having ties to the police, I thought it might be a better bet to come to you for help."

Tomas shook his head, a rough laugh escaping, before he let go of her hair and moved back, just enough so that her front wasn't plastered to his chest anymore. When she didn't drop her hand from his chest, he realized she was stroking the pad of one finger over the cross he wore. The one his birth mother used to wear before her death. It was given to him the day of her funeral, and he'd never taken it off, except to change out the chain.

"First of all, while we don't like to capture the attention of the police, we sure as hell aren't afraid of them," he said, watching her closely. "Secondly, don't ever do anything so stupid as to walk up to the fucking mafia and ask for help again. That's a good way to get a bullet in your head."

"Tomas, no!"

Ignoring his mother, Tomas placed his hand over Salome's where it rested on his chest. "This time, you were lucky. I promised my Mamá I would keep you safe if I thought you were innocent. That is what I am going to do."

Those captivating eyes filled with tears again, and then she was wiping at them with her free hand. "Thank you, Tomas. I just need your protection for a little while. Just until I can get back on my feet again and figure out who the devil is that is after me."

When Salome laid her head against the back of the couch, facing him with those big green eyes, Tomas felt something shift in his heart, a place no one except his family had been able to reach since his mother died. Glancing over at his father, his brow furrowed as he asked the question he knew the rest of his family was wondering too. "What exactly do you plan on doing once you find out who he is, sweetheart?" For some reason, the term of endearment rolled easily off his tongue when it came to this woman—it was a word he'd never used before.

"I'm going to find him and take a page from your playbook," she whispered, exhaustion heavy in her voice.

"What does that mean?" he asked, although he was sure he already knew, and no part of him liked it.

"I'll refuse to go to him. I won't let anyone take me against my will. I just need a little time."

Her voice was softer, and he knew she was struggling to stay awake, but he found he couldn't let it go. "I've told you that I am going to keep you safe, Salome. No one will take you against your will."

"No, he won't," she whispered. "I'm going to figure out who he is, find him, and then kill him."

"Have you ever killed before, Salome?"

Her little nose scrunched, but she didn't open her eyes as she whispered, "No. Although, I wanted to kill my brothers last night. Jerks."

Tomas chuckled, shaking his head. "Yeah, I've definitely wanted to kill your oldest brother myself many times before."

A soft sigh passed her lips as Salome moved closer to him. "Please don't kill him, Tomas. He's my familia, and I still love him."

"Even if the bastard doesn't deserve it," Mateo muttered.

At the sound of Mateo's voice, Salome seemed to struggle to wake up, but Tomas had heard all that he needed to for now. Slipping an arm around her waist, he pulled her closer until her head dropped to his chest. "Sleep, Salome. You are safe. No one is going to hurt you. As of right now, you are under De La Vega protection. I won't let anything, or anyone, harm you."

"Tomas," she breathed his name, and then he felt her give in. He bit back a groan as she snuggled closer to him, the feel of her soft body waking up his cock, something he did not need in the middle of a meeting with his entire family.

"What are we going to do?" Sofia asked softly. "We can't send that poor girl back to her family. And we can't allow her to kill the man who is after her. She doesn't need blood on her hands."

"I told you I would protect her," Tomas said, shifting awkwardly as he tried to make Salome more comfortable.

"I know, Tomas, and I know you will keep your promise, but I worry."

"About what, Love?" Miguel asked, picking up her hand to place a kiss against her palm.

"She says she has no idea what her family is involved in, and I believe her."

"So do I," Tomas agreed. "She's telling the truth."

"You're sure?" Miguel asked, his eyes on Tomas.

Tomas didn't hesitate. "Positive."

Miguel nodded slowly. "Yes, I agree. Do you think her brothers would really hand her over to someone who would hurt her? I don't care for Fabio Villanueva at all.

That conniving bastard doesn't have a trustworthy or loyal bone in his body, but I don't get that same impression from his boys. From what I've seen, they seem to have more honor. They have always shown respect to me, even when Fabio has not."

"I agree," Javier stated, rising from the couch to walk over to a small bar behind them. "Gio is a good man. I've spoken to him a few times. Although, he's never mentioned a sister before."

"None of them have," Mateo said, rising to follow his brother over to the bar. "And I agree; as much as I dislike the bastards, it's more because of their father and the fact that they are our competition more than anything else."

"Eh, they aren't really competition. They run guns, not drugs."

Tomas nodded slowly, knowing his father was right. They weren't competition on that front, but in others, such as power, they just might be. "Well, I say there is only one way to find out what their thoughts on this situation are."

"What way might that be, brother?" Javier asked, handing Tomas the tumbler of smooth bourbon he preferred over anything else. Tomas took a swig of the Jack, loving the way it burned down his throat, before placing it on the end table next to him.

Tomas grinned, reaching down to fish his phone out of his front pocket. "Let's call them."

"You want to call Salome's family and tell them where she is, Tomas?" Sofia demanded. "What is wrong with you? What if they show up here for her?"

"What if they do?" Tomas asked, searching through his phone for Kain's number. He'd done a few transactions with the man in the past, even though he preferred not to because of Fabio. The head of the Villanueva family was a whiny little dick. No one wanted to deal with him, so most of them went through his second, Kain.

"We can't let them have her," Sofia insisted angrily. "I won't allow you to give that girl back to them!"

Tomas hit send on his phone, putting it on speaker, then looked over at his mother. "You're right, Mamá. They cannot have her back. They don't deserve her."

Sofia stared at him, her hazel eyes lit with anger, and then she gave a short nod of satisfaction. "Good."

"What do you want, De La Vega?" Kain snarled when he picked up the line. "I'm a little fucking busy here."

"Doing what? Looking for your sister?" Tomas asked, wasting no time and cutting straight to the chase.

There was silence and then he heard Kain say, "I need to take this outside, Father. The De La Vega familia is looking for some business."

"Hurry the fuck up," Fabio snapped in the background. "We need to find that little bitch before we are all dead."

"This won't take long."

Cold, hard anger hit at the sound of the unfeeling bastard. "You let the bastard talk like that about your sister?" Tomas growled. "Your familia?"

"You don't understand."

"You're fucking right, I don't understand."

Tomas was aware of Salome stirring in his arms, and he clamped a hand over her mouth to keep her from speaking. Her eyes sprang open, wide with fear, but when she saw he was the one holding her, she began to relax. Then she heard her brother's voice.

"Look, Tomas, my father is a heartless son of a bitch, but it's my job as his second to back him."

Salome tried to squirm out of his arms, but Tomas held her tight, shaking his head.

"It's your job as his second to let him know when he's fucking up," Mateo said, walking over to stand by them. "You might want to pass that message on now."

"Dammit, you don't know the whole story."

"I know your sister is here asking for our protection because her brothers are pussies and can't take care of her themselves," Javier stated, getting in on the conversation. "Don't worry, though. We'll take care of her."

"You lay one hand on Salome, and I will tear you the fuck apart."

Salome's eyes widened, her eyes flying to meet Tomas'. He saw hurt in them, but also hope.

"I find that funny," Tomas said, removing his hand from her mouth and reaching up to tug gently on her hair, "when just a few hours ago you were ready to hand her over to someone else."

Kain sighed heavily. "She did hear that, then?"

"Fuck yeah, she heard it. Said her youngest brother, Gio, was the only one with enough balls to stand up for her."

"Shit." Kain was quiet for a moment, then he said gruffly, "Look, I know she probably won't believe me, and I wouldn't blame her, but Dario and I were just blowing smoke up our father's ass until we could figure a way to get her out of here. We were going to send her out through the tunnels, but by the time Gio got to her room, he could tell she had already been there and gone."

"What tunnels?" Salome asked in confusion before Tomas could stop her.

"Salome?"

When her gaze met his, Tomas shrugged. Her brother had already heard her voice, so it didn't matter now. Besides, he knew what he needed to know. She was more important to her brothers than she thought. For that, they would live. Tomas had promised her his protection, and that meant he would need to eliminate any threats toward her. Right now, her father was at the top of the list.

"What tunnels are you talking about?" Salome asked again, her body beginning to shake against him. "And what did you mean when you said you are Father's second? What kind of business are you in?"

"The kind you don't want to know about, Sis," Kain muttered.

"And the tunnels?"

"They run below the house. We smuggle things in and out that way."

"Why didn't I know any of this was going one?" Salome whispered. "How could I have been so blind?"

"We didn't want you to know. We hid it from you. All of it. Hold on a second. Someone's coming."

"Kain, Father wants you back in there," someone said, so clearly, they could hear them through the phone.

"Giovanni," Salome whispered, her hand going out as if to touch the phone.

"I'm busy," Kain told him. "I'm brokering a deal and you know how much we need the money."

"Yeah, well screw the money. If I go back in there right now, I'm liable to put a bullet in his fucking head after what he did to my sister. So, unless you want him dead, I suggest you move."

A tremulous smile crossed Salome's lips when she

heard what her younger brother said, a look of pure love shining in her eyes.

"Give the phone to Gio and go talk to your father," Tomas ordered, knowing at that moment that every word that had come out of Salome's mouth had been the truth. Not that he had doubted her before, but now he had proof. For some reason, it mattered more to him than it should.

"Look, Tomas."

"Give him the fucking phone."

"Is that Tomas De La Vega?" they heard Gio ask in a hushed tone. "Is Javier there? That man is a wizard with a computer. Maybe he can help us find Salome."

"Gio."

"I'll pay him myself," Gio interrupted. "Whatever he wants."

"Just take the damn phone," Kain grunted.

There was a rustling, then they heard, "De La Vega, this is Giovanni Villanueva."

"Hey Gio," Javier called out. "This is Javier. You trying to track down someone?"

"Hold on." They heard more rustling, then a door shut. "Yeah, I need to find my sister, Salome. I'll pay whatever you want. Fuck, I'll give you my life. My life for hers. I don't give a shit, but I need you to find her before my father, or that bastard he promised her to, does."

"Two questions first."

"Whatever it takes."

"How come we never knew you had a sister?"

Gio sighed. "Cause, she's too good for this life, man. She's the light to all of our darkness." Tears fell from Salome's eyes as her brother went on. "She runs our restaurants. I seriously don't think they will survive without her, not that I give a shit. Her safety means more than our restaurants to me. But we don't flaunt the fact that she's our sister to everyone because we want to keep her safe. We would all give our lives for her, even though she probably doesn't think that now, but it's the truth." He paused for a second before saying, "Well, all except our father. He's a fucking dick. Treats her like shit. Makes her work like a dog, tells her what she can or can't wear, won't let her have any friends. We've tried to make up for that over the years—tried to make her happy, but I don't know if we succeeded or not."

"What about your father?" Mateo asked. "Why does he keep her a secret if he doesn't care for her the way you do?"

"Who the fuck is this?"

"It's my brother, Mateo," Javier said. "We're all here: Mateo, Tomas, me, and my father."

"Shit."

"That answers the part about why your brothers do it, but why does Fabio keep her a secret?" Mateo pressed.

"Because she makes us vulnerable," Gio said finally. "While it might not affect him, it does affect all three of her brothers, which means it makes him vulnerable as well."

"One more question," Javier said.

"You said two," Gio growled.

"One more."

"Fine," Gio conceded darkly. "Make it fast. I need to get back in there."

"First of all, if I find your sister, will you kneel before me and let me put a bullet in your head without a fight?"

"Yes." There was no hesitation in Gio's reply—no

58

wavering. "You find her, I will gladly give you my life. Just… give me time to eliminate the threat to her first. Let me take him out, then I'm yours."

"Which brings me to our last question," Tomas, his voice a low growl. "Who is the person who is a threat to her?"

This time Gio did hesitate. "He's powerful, De La Vega. Maybe even more powerful than you and your family."

"But you are going after him?" Javier asked.

"I will do whatever I have to for my sister."

"Oh, Gio," Salome said, grasping Tomas' hand that held the phone tightly. "I'm here. I'm already with the De La Vega family. I'm safe."

"Salome?" There was silence, and then, "Is it really you?"

Tomas heard the hope and worry in the man's voice that Gio didn't try to hide. "Yeah, it's her," he told him. "Showed up on our doorstep an hour or so ago asking for protection. Now, answer the second question. Who is the threat to her?"

"You take care of my sister. I will handle him."

Salome's eyes widened, and she shook her head emphatically as she clutched tightly to him.

"I don't think you understand, Son," Miguel said. "This is Don De La Vega. My family has given our protection to your sister, this means we will eliminate any threat to her ourselves. Give us the name. Now."

"But, why would you do that?" Gio asked in confusion.

"Because I choose to," Miguel replied.

"Our Don would never do something like that," Gio muttered.

"Your Don is a coward."

"Gio, where the hell are you? We gotta roll!"

"Shit," Gio whispered, "I have to go. Take care of my sister. Tell her…"

"She can hear you," Tomas said quietly.

"It's okay, Gio," Salome murmured, "I love you, and I forgive you—all of you."

"I want a name before you go, Son," the Don ordered. "It would be in your best interest to comply."

They heard the sound of someone beating on a door, before Gio whispered, "The Devil, Diego Valdez." Then he was gone.

"Well, this just went from bad to totally fucked," Javier said, slapping the couch next to him.

Tomas let go of Salome and rose from the couch, grabbing his glass of Jack. Throwing back his head, he drank the rest of it down in one gulp, trying to push back the memories that came flooding forth at the sound of Diego Valdez's name—the man who had murdered his mother.

"Tomas? What's wrong?" Salome asked, and he hated the fear he heard in her voice, which told him he was in trouble. Hell, he'd just met the woman, and he was already wanting to fight the world for her. What was wrong with him?

"I've got to get out of here," he growled, slamming the glass down so hard on the end table, he was surprised it didn't break.

"I don't understand," Salome whispered.

Tomas couldn't answer. He had to leave now, before he

showed Salome a side of himself that would really terrify her.

"Just let him have some space," he heard Sofia say as he left the room. He didn't look back. He had to go— needed to hit something—needed to beat the shit out of something. Which was how he found himself down in the basement gym fifteen minutes later, pounding away at a bag hanging from the ceiling, the skin of his knuckles torn open and bleeding.

He was going to do what he should have done years ago. Find Valdez and end him.

CHAPTER EIGHT

S alome walked out onto the balcony of the bedroom she'd been given the night she arrived, staring up at the stars in the dark sky. The long, pale blue nightgown she wore billowed out around her in the chilly night wind. Her hair was loose, hanging halfway down her back in waves of black and deep red silk. She shivered, wrapping her arms around her waist as she blinked back tears.

It was just over a week since she came to the villa, and true to their word, the De La Vega family had kept her safe. Not only that, but they fed her, clothed her, and gave her a large bedroom with a bathroom for privacy.

It had been quiet. No sound from her family, the police, or Diego Valdez. She missed her brothers, and she missed work, probably because that was all she really knew. She was starting to go a little stir crazy, but she refused to go out and possibly endanger the people who had taken her in when they didn't have to.

Salome had eaten breakfast in the kitchen with the staff the morning after she arrived, and then it became a habit to share all of her meals with them. Except for dinners, which she ate with Miguel and Sofia in the large dining room. Normally, Mateo and Javier joined them, but never the one man she really wanted to see—the one who caught her attention when they first met, and who consumed her thoughts during the day.

If she was honest, a part of her was disappointed because after that first day, she'd only seen Tomas a couple of times, and not once had he spoken more than a casual hello to her. She had no idea where he'd been, but she wasn't going to ask in case she didn't want to hear the answer. For all she knew, he was married or had a girl-friend. Just because he promised to protect her and had held her when she was scared, didn't mean he wanted anything more from her. And why did the idea of him seeing someone bother her so much? She did not have time for a De La Vega male in her life right now. Hell, she didn't have time for any man. She needed to concentrate on finding out who was after her. The problem was, she had no idea how to do that.

Deciding she needed something to do to take her mind off Tomas, Salome went back into her room and grabbed a robe off the closet door. Sliding her arms into the silky sleeves, she tied the sash and then picked up the book she'd borrowed from the huge library the day before that was just down the hall from her room. She'd already finished it and needed something new.

Leaving the bedroom, Salome walked down the hall quietly. It was after two in the morning, a time when most people would already be in bed, and she didn't want to wake anyone up. In this house, that would probably be a good way to find a knife to her throat.

Opening the library door, she slipped inside, then closed it softly behind her. Too late, she realized the light was on and she wasn't alone. Swinging around, she stiffened when she saw the man she'd just been obsessing over sitting in a chair by the window, a glass of whiskey on the small table beside him. When their eyes met, she flushed nervously, then bit her lower lip as she looked away.

"Can't sleep?" Tomas asked, laying the book he'd been reading down on the table.

Slowly, Salome shook her head. She'd barely slept since she arrived. It was hard to when all she thought about when she closed her eyes was Diego Valdez, wondering who he was and when he would be coming for her. No one would tell her anything, except that he was an evil man she never wanted to meet, and that she didn't need to worry, they would handle everything. While she appreciated the fact that they had promised their protection, she still wanted more information about him.

Turning, Salome crossed the room to replace the book from where she'd taken it the day before, blindly grabbing one off a shelf below it so she could get out of there. As much as she wanted to be in his presence, she didn't think Tomas felt the same. If he did, he would have sought her out before now, wouldn't he?

"Salome?"

Stiffening, Salome glanced over at him, suddenly wishing she was anywhere but there. "Yes?"

"Do you really want to read that one?"

Looking down, her eyes narrowed on the book she'd chosen, and a harsh laugh escaped before she could stop it. A book on amphibians. No, she had no desire to read about frogs or toads, or any other slimy thing. And she had just made herself look like a complete fool.

Shaking her head, Salome stalked back over to the bookshelf and returned it, not bothering to grab another one before heading back toward the door and opening it. "Night, Tomas."

He said her name again, but she just kept walking. She had to get the hell out of there. What was wrong with her? She wasn't the type of person who couldn't form a complete sentence around a man she was interested in. She was a strong, capable woman who ran eight successful restaurants, for fuck's sake.

Salome groaned as she let herself back into her room. Why was she so attracted to Tomas De La Vega? She didn't even know him. She had only really spoken to him on the day she arrived. Maybe it had something to do with the fact that he'd promised to protect her and held her in his arms, things no one else had ever done to her in her entire life. Her white knight. But where the hell had he been the past ten days if he was supposed to be keeping her safe? He couldn't do that if he wasn't around.

She sighed, crossing the room to remove her robe and hang it back up. Chances were, he was probably avoiding her. For some reason, the name Diego Valdez had pissed him off and sent him out of the room that day, away from her, but no one would tell her why. She'd tentatively broached the subject with Sofia one night, but had been shut down quickly. Sofia said it wasn't her story to tell, but there'd been no way to miss the pain in the other woman's eyes. Maybe it wasn't hers, but Salome would bet money, that it somehow involved her.

Salome was lost in thought and didn't realize that she

wasn't alone until she heard the loud click of a door being shut behind her. Swinging around, she froze when she saw Tomas standing just a few feet away, staring at her intently. "What's wrong, Salome?" When she only shook her head but didn't reply, he took a step toward her. "What did I tell you that first day we met, woman?"

"I don't know what you are talking about."

"We will not have a relationship built on lies. I asked you a question, and I expect an honest answer."

Salome crossed her arms over her chest, glaring at him. She was unaware of the way the movement pushed up the bodice of her nightgown, showing a substantial amount of cleavage until his eyes lowered... and stayed.

"What relationship, Tomas?" she demanded, ignoring that part of her that was reveling in the way his eyes were glued to her breasts. "I've hardly seen you since I arrived."

"I've been busy."

"Doing what?" she snapped, knowing she was being unreasonable, but unable to stop. "You promised to protect me, but you haven't been around to do it."

"I have been protecting you," he growled, tearing his gaze from her chest as he began to slowly stalk across the room in her direction.

"How, by avoiding me?"

"What the hell are you talking about, Salome?"

"You've barely said two words to me in the past week and a half, Tomas."

"I've been busy."

Resting her hands on her hips, Salome arched an eyebrow as she asked, "Oh yeah? Busy doing what, or is it who?" The second the words left her lips, she felt like a jealous little bitch who had no right in the world to be jealous of anyone or anything connected to Tomas De La Vega. Holding up a hand before he could reply, she said, "Please, forget those words came out of my mouth. You don't know me. Not really. You owe me nothing, not even the protection you extended my way."

He stared at her in silence, making her feel like an idiot, before she turned away from him and stalked over to stand in front of the balcony window.

"Salome."

"Please, just go... wherever it is that you go."

She jumped when she felt his arms go around her waist, pulling her back flush against his body. A low moan slipped out when she felt the hard length of his cock pressing into her ass. His hands moved up to cup her breasts, and he thrust against her. "Fuck, you feel good."

Salome tilted her head back against his shoulder, another moan escaping when he began to knead her breasts, rubbing his thumbs over her nipples. She wanted this man—needed him. Which was crazy. She didn't even know him. It didn't matter. Her body was calling the shots, and it was saying that the thick length pressing into her backside needed to be buried deep inside her... now.

"Your brother was right," Tomas rasped, lowering his hands to stroke them down over her hips. Grasping them, he pressed his hard cock into her again as he placed hot kisses over her shoulder.

"Can we not talk about my brother right now?" Salome whispered, reaching up to sweep her hair from her neck to give him better access.

"He was right, Salome. You are better than this life. I don't want this for you."

Salome turned to face him, her hands going to his

chest. She slid them up to his shoulders, moving in closer. "Is that why you stayed away?"

Tomas slid his hand into her hair, cradling the back of her head, forcing her head up to meet his eyes. "I don't do this, Salome."

"Do what?" she gasped when he cupped her ass with his other hand and pulled her up into his hard, thick cock.

"I'm a hard man. I don't share my emotions with women. I fuck them, and then I leave. That's it. I've never met a woman I wanted more with."

Salome's gaze roamed over the face of the man in front of her, his eyes dark with a desire and a possessiveness she wasn't sure he was aware of. She wanted more than one night with him, even knowing she shouldn't, but if one night was all he was willing to give, then it would have to be enough. Nodding slowly, she whispered, "I understand."

"No, I don't think you do," he said, his eyes falling to her lips. "I can't stop thinking about you, Salome. About the way you would taste if I kissed you. How soft your skin would feel if I touched it the way I wanted to. How it would feel to be balls deep inside you." Lowering his head, his eyes still on her lips, he growled, "I stayed away to keep you safe. From me."

"Don't I get a say?" There was no way in hell she was backing away from this man. She didn't want to play it safe. She wanted him.

"Stop me, Salome, because if I do get a taste of those lips, I may not ever let you go," he rasped, his mouth just a breath away now.

"What happened to fucking and leaving?" she whispered softly, her arms going up around his neck.

"That's what I'm trying to tell you, sweetheart. There will be fucking, but there will be no leaving. Not anytime soon, if ever."

"Can we get on with the fucking part?" she teased, one hand going up to stroke over his smooth, bald head.

"Salome," he groaned, his hand tightening in her hair. "I'm not a good man."

That might be what he thought, but she also knew different. While his parents may not have discussed some things with her, they had shared many stories about their sons' lives over the years that had shown her what kind of men they were. She knew what she needed to know.

"Maybe not, but you are my man," she said, right before fusing their mouths together.

Tomas groaned, his hand in her hair, holding her still as he took over. His tongue traced her lips, then slipped past them inside her mouth, finding hers. He licked, stroked, and sucked, swallowing her moans of pleasure.

Wanting to feel his skin against hers, Salome grasped his T-shirt in her hands and slid it up, breaking their kiss long enough to help him shrug out of it. Her hands went to his jogging pants next, sliding them down over his hips before dropping to her knees to help him take them the rest of the way off. She licked her lips, her eyes on the long, thick cock in front of her, and then with a soft moan, she leaned forward to lick him from the base all the way to the tip.

"Fuck, Salome, you do that, and this isn't going to last very long," he warned, both hands now buried in her hair as he held her still.

Meeting his gaze, she let a slow smile cross her face as she licked around the head of his dick, and then lowered her head down, taking in as much of him as she could, before coming back up. Twirling her tongue around the tip, she moaned as she tasted a drop of pre-cum.

"I want to fuck that pretty mouth," Tomas growled, pushing just the head of his cock past her lips. "I love the way your lips look around my dick. So hot. I want you to take it all."

Salome's eyes widened at the thought of him taking control, and a shot of excitement raced through her. Her pussy was hot, wet, and begging for his touch, but she ignored it. For now, this was about him and giving him what he needed.

When Tomas began to push deeper inside, Salome opened for him, showing him that she was on board. "I don't want to hurt you," he whispered, clutching her hair in his hands as he began slow, shallow thrusts. She raised her hands to his ass, digging her nails in, trying to let him know that he wasn't hurting her. Moaning, she sucked him harder, taking him deeper, licking at his cock when he pulled back out.

"Shit, Salome!"

He began to move in and out of her mouth faster, going deeper than before, but never enough to actually hurt her. He held her still as he moved, and the small bite of pain turned her on even more. When she couldn't hold back any longer, she reached down and pulled her nightgown up, sticking her hand inside her wet panties to find her clit. While Tomas controlled her mouth, she controlled her clit until he figured out what she was doing.

"You like that, baby?" he groaned, thrusting one more time before pulling out of her mouth. "You like to touch yourself?"

"I'd rather you touched me," she admitted, rising to her feet and wrapping a hand around his dick.

"Me too," he rasped, grasping the sides of her night-gown then sliding it up over her body and off. Her panties were next before he was on his knees before her. His tongue found her clit, stroking over it quickly, as he slipped one finger inside her and then another. "You are so ready for me."

"Yes," Salome cried, riding his fingers as she chased the orgasm that was close to combustion. "Tomas!"

He ate at her, licking and sucking her clit as he thrust his fingers in and out. She clutched at his shoulders, plea-sure racing through her. Then she was going over the edge, his name on her lips over and over as she erupted.

Tomas rose quickly, lifting her in his arms and carrying her to the bed. Laying her down, he followed her, lifting her legs up slightly as he pressed the head of his cock to her entrance. He stopped, locking his gaze with hers. "This is your last chance to say no, Salome."

In response, she slipped her legs around him, pressing her heels into his ass, and arched up. She moaned when he sank slowly into her, stopping a couple of times so she could adjust to his thickness. She'd only had sex twice in her life, and neither time had felt like this. Wild, hot, excit-ing. She hadn't even had an orgasm before, except by her own hand.

"You feel so good, sweetheart. So tight and hot. Perfect."

Tomas began to move slowly, one hand clasped with hers above her head, the other holding onto her hip. Salome matched him thrust for thrust, panting softly as she closed her eyes and just allowed herself to feel. Soon, he was thrusting deeper, faster, harder, and it wasn't long before she fell over the edge again, Tomas following this time.

"That was amazing," Salome murmured, her eyes closing as exhaustion began to beat at her.

"Yeah, it was," Tomas agreed quietly, slipping out of her and rolling to the side before pulling her close.

"Don't go," she whispered, snuggling close to him, her hand sliding through the hair on his chest to rest on the gold cross that sat there.

"Not until in the morning," he promised, kissing her forehead gently. "I have a meeting with the Don I can't miss."

"Okay." Salome slowly drifted off to sleep in his arms, feeling completely safe for the first time since she'd ran from her father's house.

CHAPTER NINE

"Profits are already up since Raul took over. He's good at what he does and is loyal to our familia."

"I agree," Miguel said, leaning forward in his chair, his arms resting on the desk in front of him. "Give him a ten percent raise. He has a large family to support."

"Yes, Father."

"How is your search for Valdez going?" Miguel asked, turning his attention from Mateo to Tomas.

Tomas met his hard gaze, anger boiling in him at the thought of Diego Valdez. When Salome had told them the man after her had been referred to as the Devil, never once had he thought she meant Diego. The man had been given that name just a few years after he murdered Tomas' mother, a result of a killing spree he went on, taking out three prominent families in Colombia. He'd gone underground after that, only showing himself sporadically. Still, he believed himself to be untouchable. Tomas was looking forward to showing him just how wrong he was. Not only for his mother, but for Salome.

"I've been tracking him with Javier's help. It's taking time, but we will find him soon. There is nowhere he can hide from us."

"And once you find him?"

"Is that even a question?" It wasn't in his mind. He was a threat to the woman who now owned him after last night. If the bastard ever got his hands on her, he would break her, and there was no way in hell Tomas was going to let that happen.

Miguel nodded, sliding his chair away from his desk. "Let me know when you find him, and what you need to take him down."

"He needs his brothers," Mateo said, rising to his feet. "We will be there."

"Damn straight," Javier said, kicking away from the wall he was leaning against. "Familia sticks together."

"Familia," Mateo said, stepping closer to them and holding his fist out.

"Familia," Tomas repeated, bumping fists with his brothers, before turning and walking to the door.

"Hey, where are you going?" Javier demanded.

"To find my woman."

"What?" Javier asked in confusion. "You have a woman? Since when?"

"Since she showed up at our gate a week and a half ago," Mateo said, striding past them. "Where have you been, Javier?"

"Salome?"

Tomas grinned, following his brother to the door. "Yep."

"Well, shit, I guess I'll go track down the Devil by my fucking self."

"Let me know when you find him," Tomas replied, his thoughts already on the beautiful brunette that he was tracking down.

"Tomas, wait."

Tomas stopped, looking back at Miguel. "You need me, Father?" It didn't matter how much he wanted to get to Salome, he would always answer to the Don first.

Miguel waved his other sons out and then motioned toward the door. "Close it. Let's talk."

Tomas stiffened, unsure where this conversation was going, but he obeyed. Shutting the door, he moved back over and took a seat in front of his father's desk. "I'm listening."

Miguel nodded, scooting his chair back up to his desk and resting his elbows on it, steepling his fingers together. "Son, I'm going to tell you something that not many others know, not even Sofia, and I would like to keep it that way. You may share this with Salome, but no other. Not even your brothers. Understand?"

Tomas frowned, not liking the thought of keeping things from Mateo and Javier. The only secrets he kept from them were the locations of the bodies he'd hidden over time, and that was for their own safety.

Miguel held up a hand, a small smile appearing. "I can see where your mind is going, Tomas, and this is nothing horrendous. But it is something that could hurt the members of our family, and I have no wish to do that."

Tomas slowly nodded, relaxing back against his seat. "Understood."

"As you already know," Miguel started, a faraway look appearing in his eyes, "Sofia and I were married before I met your mother. What you don't know, is that ours was an arranged marriage, one I was very much against."

No, he hadn't known that.

"Our fathers set it up, wanting to join our familias together and grow our organization. However, Sofia's father and mother, along with her brothers, were murdered less than a month into our marriage. Which meant we were stuck in a union that neither of us wanted."

"Neither of you?" Tomas asked in confusion. They'd always seemed so in love.

"Yes, but Sofia had nowhere to go, and I couldn't just kick her out. Her familia was dead, there was no one to support and take care of her. Any money they had was absorbed by the new Don that took over after her father's death. So, we came to an agreement. We would keep up our sham of a marriage, be civil to one another, but be apart. We lived in the same house, but in separate bedrooms next to each other. We took our meals together, spent holidays together, and were always civil to one another."

"I had no idea." Things began to make more sense as the story unfolded, and Tomas began to see everything about their past in a new light.

"No one did, not even our staff. Sofia and I kept our true feelings a secret, which wasn't hard to do… until I met Antonela."

Tomas clenched his teeth together tightly at the mention of his birth mother.

"When a De La Vega falls for a woman, he falls hard, Tomas. That's how it is in our family, and it was part of the reason I fought against a union with Sofia. She was a sweet, caring, beautiful woman when we met, but the idea of being forced into something when I knew I could have what my parents had, what their parents had, just pissed me off. I didn't want to settle, but I felt like I had no choice."

Another piece of the puzzle fell into place. Tomas had always wondered how a man as noble as his father, one loyal to family and full of honor, could do what he did to Sofia. It didn't mesh with the father he knew and loved. But, if he felt the way about Tomas' mother that Tomas did for Salome in such a short time, it was beginning to make sense.

"I met Antonela just over a year after Sofia and I were married. She was so vibrant and full of life. She caught my eye the moment she walked into the restaurant where I was meeting with your Uncle Tito. She was on the arm of Samuel Valdez, our sworn enemy, but it didn't matter. The minute my gaze locked on her; I was lost. There wasn't anything I wouldn't have done to have her. It was at that moment, that I realized what the rest of my family meant when they said a De La Vega falls fast and hard."

As much as Tomas loved to hear about his birth mother, a part of him felt disloyal to the woman who had raised him since he was five years old, loving him as her own son. But it didn't stop him from leaning forward in his chair to hang on every word.

"I am not proud of the way I handled things," Miguel went on, "but I wouldn't change it either. It gave me six years with the woman who held my soul, and it gave me a son I am beyond proud to call mine."

"If my mother held your soul, how did Sofia end up with your heart?" Tomas asked curiously, because there was no doubt in his mind that the woman he called mother now, was loved by the man sitting in front of him.

The Don's face softened the way it did only when speaking of his wife, a small smile filled with love appearing. "Ah, what you need to understand, my son, is that while you may give your soul to one woman and never get it back, your heart can be given to someone else. Fortunately, I was lucky enough to have my soul returned to me after your mother's death, so that I could share both of them with my Sofia." Tapping his fingers on the desk, Miguel seemed to be collecting his thoughts before he went on, "After I lost Antonela, I brought you home. I had thought to hire a nanny to raise you, but the moment Sofia found out what happened, she refused to let that happen. She said things were going to change. That a child needed a mother, a familia, and that was exactly what you were going to get."

Tomas felt a smile forming as he thought about the way Sofia had accepted him right away. Back then, he was too young to realize what it meant that Sofia was his father's wife and his mother his mistress. All he knew was that he'd lost the one person who had been constant in his life, but someone had stepped in to take over that role, showing him just as much love as he'd been given by his own mother.

"I was devastated at the time, and grateful to Sofia for taking over. She gave me six months to grieve, and then set down the law, like only Sofia can do." Miguel chuckled, shaking his head. "I had no idea she had it in her, but she told me there would be no more stepping out on her, which I hadn't done with anyone except Antonela. She decided that we were going to have a real marriage, and she wanted more children—that you needed siblings. It didn't take the woman long to steal my heart after I finally opened up to her, and my soul soon followed."

Tomas nodded in understanding. He would say Salome held his soul now, but not quite yet his heart. He was sure it wouldn't be long before she captured that, too.

Miguel stood, coming around the desk and clapping a hand on Tomas' shoulder. "I am sure you understand why it would be a bad idea to let Sofia find out that someone else owned my soul before her, correct? I've never explained it to her the way I did to you. And your brothers do not need to know that part either. When it is their time, I will explain, but not about Antonela."

"I agree."

"And Salome?"

"I've wanted her since the day we met," Tomas admitted. "It is just like you said. She owns me."

Miguel nodded, squeezing his shoulder. "Good, Son. That is good. Sofia and I like her. She will make a fine addition to the familia."

"I never said I was marrying her," Tomas interjected, rising to his feet.

"You would disrespect her like that?" Miguel challenged, his eyes narrowing dangerously on him.

Tomas grinned, shaking his head. "Never, but she might reject me someday when I ask her."

Miguel's eyes lit up with laughter and he shook his head. "Not if what we heard through the walls early this morning, is anything to go by."

CHAPTER TEN

"So, what you are saying, is that the date didn't go as planned?" Salome teased her new friend, Luciana Reyes, as she popped another grape into her mouth. She'd met the woman when she found the kitchen the first morning she'd eaten breakfast at the villa and had instantly liked her.

"Not at all, child. My daughter is headstrong, sassy as they come, and not afraid to tell you what she thinks, which sometimes is not the best combination. It was over the moment that ass opened his mouth and told her what he thought of women working outside the home, but she didn't just walk out of the place. No, not my Katsya."

"What did she do?" Salome asked, eagerly anticipating the answer. She hadn't met Katsya Reyes before, but after everything Luciana had told her, she really wanted to.

"Well, let's just say, he was picking himself up off the floor moments later, after her fist connected with his jaw." A small smile appeared as Luciana shook her head. "The things my Raul teaches our girls! I swear!"

Salome laughed, feeling slightly envious of the life Katsya and her sisters must have grown up in with parents like Raul and Luciana. She missed out on having a mother around who loved her, and a father who doted on her. She wondered what that would have felt like. Shaking off her thoughts, she grinned. "I don't know. I would have given anything to see Katsya knock that fool on his ass."

"Oh, really?" a deep voice said from the kitchen doorway. "Would you like to learn to do something like that, sweetheart?"

Salome felt her face flush at the sound of Tomas' voice, and her heart began to race as she looked in his direction. "I would like to learn to defend myself, yes."

"You have me to protect you," he countered, crossing the room and sliding his arms around her waist.

Her breath caught as she returned his gaze, surprised that he seemed to be staking his claim on her in front of others.

"This is true, but there may be times that you can't be there to protect me, Tomas. It would be nice to know that I could pull a Katsya and knock a guy down if he came at me."

"A Katsya?"

Luciana chuckled as she picked up Salome's now empty plate and put it in the sink. "Katsya is our oldest daughter. She has quite the right hook on her."

"Hmmm, maybe it would be best if you stay away from this woman, Salome. We don't want her putting any ideas into your head."

When Salome glared at him in reply, Tomas threw his head back and laughed, a deep rich sound that filled the air and put a look of shock on Luciana's face. Salome ignored it. She knew from what she'd seen so far, and what his parents had told her, that Tomas wasn't one for joking and fun. He was the more quiet, serious one of the De La Vega brothers. Maybe it was time that changed. "I don't know, Tomas," she teased, "I am thinking I might hire her to train me."

He scowled at her, shaking his head. "You don't need anyone to train you in anything except for me, Salome."

"You will teach me how to throw a punch? How to defend myself?"

His scowl darkening, Tomas pulled her closer to him. "You really want to learn, sweetheart?"

Salome was aware of Luciana discreetly leaving the room, as she replied. "Yes, I do."

Slowly, he nodded, as he gently cupped her jaw in his hand. "Then I will, but first, I need to taste you again."

A soft moan slipped out when his mouth touched hers. She clutched tightly to the front of his shirt as he teased her lips with his tongue. Her hands crept up around his neck, pulling him closer, while his hands moved down to cup her ass and pull her into his thickening erection.

"We have fifty rooms in this house," Mateo said as he walked into the kitchen. "Find a different one."

Tomas flipped his brother off, taking his time to remove his lips from hers. "Maybe I should have this Reyes woman show you how to pull her Katsya move," he muttered, giving her one last quick kiss. "You can test it out on Mateo."

"Oh, yes, please! That would be fun!"

"What the hell are you talking about?" Mateo demanded, glowering at them.

Salome giggled, then slapped her hand over her mouth,

her eyes widening. What the hell? She was a grown ass woman. She did not giggle like a teenage girl.

"My woman is going to take some self-defense lessons from Raul Reyes' daughter," Tomas said, winking at her. "Then, she's going to try them out on you."

"Good luck with that," Mateo muttered, grabbing a water from the fridge and walking past them to leave the room.

"I don't know, Mateo," Salome said jokingly, "Luciana said Katsya put some man on his ass last night after he voiced his idiotic opinion about women in the workplace. I bet if she taught me, I could take you."

Mateo paused, glancing back at her. "I'll pay her to teach you, little one. And if you can drop me, I'll buy you an entire new wardrobe to fill your closet."

"Shoes too?" Salome asked excitedly. She missed her clothes from home. Sofia had been wonderful about getting her some outfits, but she was used to having hundreds of things to choose from. Not just a weeks' worth of items.

"Sure."

When Mateo left, Salome looked at Tomas with wide eyes. "Is he serious?"

"My brother never says anything he doesn't mean," Tomas said, shaking his head. "Looks like you better get that woman's number from her Mamá, and Mateo better pray that she isn't as good as I think she may be with Raul as her father."

Salome clapped her hands together, a wide smile spreading across her face. "Yes! This is going to be so much fun if Katsya agrees!"

Shaking his head at her, Tomas laughed. "It will be worth it, if you can put my brother on his ass."

"Sorry to interrupt, but I need your opinion on something, Tomas."

Salome glanced over as Javier entered the room, his laptop in his hands. From what she'd been told, he was the tech savvy one of the brothers. He did the background checks on all of their employees, and it was up to him to keep track of all of their purchase transactions in the organization. She still wasn't sure exactly what it was they dealt in, but she assumed it was weapons, drugs, or money laundering. Funny, the thought of it didn't terrify her like it should. She found she trusted them—all of them, not just Tomas. They had been nothing but good to her since she arrived, slowly letting her into their lives over the past few days, as she had been letting them into hers.

Figuring they would want their privacy, Salome stepped away from Tomas. "I'm going to run up to the library and see if I can find something to read."

"The amphibians didn't do anything for you?" Tomas teased.

Sending him a mock scowl, she countered, "You know damn well I put that book back, Tomas De La Vega."

A wicked grin crossed his face as he walked over to the kitchen table. Taking a seat, he motioned for his younger brother to sit next to him. "True." Holding out an arm to Salome, he said, "Come. Sit with us."

Javier's eyes flew from Tomas to her, but he didn't argue as he crossed the room to take the chair Tomas had indicated.

"Are you sure? I understand if you would prefer I leave."

"Stay." He tugged a chair over next to him, then waited patiently for her to come and lower herself into it before turning back to his brother. "Show us."

Javier glanced at her, then opened his laptop. As he waited for the screen to flash on, he said, "We've been trying to track down Diego Valdez ever since we found out he was the one after you. I find what I can on him, Tomas tracks down the lead."

"Diego went into hiding years ago. He comes out just long enough to remind everyone why they call him the Devil, and then he's gone again," Tomas told her. "He has numerous places under several different aliases. Six that Javier has found so far. I've staked out all of them in the past week but haven't found any sign of him yet."

"That's where you've been?" Salome asked, avoiding Tomas' gaze. She'd been a stupid, spiteful woman when he had been out trying to find and eliminate the threat to her, exactly as he promised.

"Yes. The sooner I find him, the sooner you will be safe."

"Wait, you go alone to these places?" Worry filled her at the thought of Tomas taking on someone like Diego Valdez by himself.

"Tomas just cases the places. If he did find Valdez at one of them, he would call us, and we would come up with a plan before we infiltrated. He wouldn't go in alone."

"I call bullshit," Salome interjected, her eyes going to the specs of a villa that Javier had pulled up on his computer now. It was large, but not near as big as the one she was currently living in.

"What?"

"Don't take me for an idiot, Javier," Salome said

coolly, turning the computer so that she could see the villa better. "You and I both know your brother wouldn't wait for anyone. For some reason, that I am not aware of, he had it out for this Valdez before I even came into the picture. There is no way Tomas is going to stand down and wait for you and the calvary to show up. He'll go in guns blazing."

Javier's eyes darkened, and he turned his intense gaze on Tomas. "Is she right, Tomas? You would go in without us?"

Salome froze, slowly turning to look at Tomas. Shit, had Javier really been in the dark? It was painfully obvious to her what Tomas would do. Why didn't his family know? Tomas looked back at her with pride, and she slowly let out the breath she hadn't even realized she was holding out.

"Yes, Salome is right. If I would have found him before today, I would have gone in on my own."

"Dammit, Tomas!" Javier shouted, slamming his hand on the table. "That's not how we do things."

Tomas shrugged, "I had a vested interest at the time. A reason to kill the bastard. Two of them, actually."

"And now?" Javier demanded angrily.

"I still have them, but I have a reason to live that trumps everything."

"I don't understand," Salome whispered, unable to tear her gaze from his.

"Two reasons to kill Diego. One, to keep you safe. Two, to avenge my mother's death." When Salome frowned in confusion, he said, "He killed my birth mother when I was five years old. Put a bullet between her eyes. I sat with her for hours before Father showed up."

"Oh, Tomas!" Salome cried, her hand going up to cover her mouth in shock. "I didn't know."

Tomas captured her hand in his and brought it to his own mouth, placing a gentle kiss on her palm. "I have wanted to avenge her death ever since I can remember, but I held back so that I didn't bring his wrath onto my family. At first, he hunted me, thinking I was his dead brother's son. Father kept me hidden for years, but eventually Diego found out who I was and that I was a De La Vega, not a Valdez."

"What did he do?" Salome asked softly.

"It's been a pissing match off and on ever since," Javier said. "He tried to kill Tomas a couple of times, but then got sidetracked with people hunting him. He went underground and never came after Tomas again. Probably figured he wasn't worth it after the last time. Tomas took out five of his best men."

"You… killed them?" Salome whispered.

"In this life, it's kill or be killed," Javier told her. "They came after him, boxed him in at one of our warehouses in the middle of the city. If Tomas hadn't gotten them first, he would be dead right now."

Salome nodded slowly, her eyes going back to the villa. She would think about the confirmation she'd just received about Tomas killing in the past later. Right now, she would try to concentrate on the Devil. "So, this is where you think he is right now?"

"Yes. It's only like three hours from here. Tomas could leave now to check it out and be back in the morning."

"I'm going with him."

Tomas' face became a hard mask, his eyes narrowing on her as he growled, "The fuck you are."

"Dammit, Tomas, this is my fight, too. I'm not going to sit around here while you put your life on the line when I can be there with you to back you up."

"This coming from the same woman who has no idea how to throw a punch?"

Salome cocked an eyebrow, tilting her head to the side as she leveled her eyes on him. "You don't need to know how to throw a punch if you know how to pull a trigger."

"You can shoot?" Tomas asked, his brow furrowing as he stared at her.

"Of course, she can, dumbass. Her family sells weapons on the black market. I'm sure her brothers showed her how to shoot."

"They what?" Salome whispered, turning her gaze to Javier. Of course, she'd known they were into something, but had no idea what. Now, it all made sense. The tunnels under the house that Kain had mentioned, the reason they called him her father's second, why they had such a huge collection of weapons in the saferoom. She frowned. Come to think of it, how many people actually had a saferoom. Shit, had she been living under a rock?

"They sell guns illegally, Salome," Tomas said, glaring over at his brother. "However, that should have been something they explained to you, not Javier."

"Does that mean that all of the restaurants are a cover for their gun smuggling?"

"Yeah," Javier said, drumming his fingers on the table in agitation. "Sorry, Salome. Tomas is right, I should have kept my mouth shut."

"So," Salome whispered, almost dreading the next question she was going to ask, "what is it that your family is in to?" Thinking they were involved with any kind of smuggling and actually knowing for a fact what they did were two different things.

Tomas and Javier exchanged glances but kept quiet.

"Seriously, you two? I know you are involved in some form of organized crime; I just don't know what. Is it weapons like my family? Drugs?" She froze when another thought occurred to her, and she pushed herself away from Tomas slightly. "Just tell me it isn't human trafficking. As long as it isn't that, I think we will be fine."

"It isn't that," a deep voice said from the doorway, and she looked over to see the Don walk into the room. "Your family is involved in weapons, ours, drugs. We make them and sell them, but we do not use them in any way, shape, or form here."

"But you sell them to whoever wants to buy them?"

Miguel shrugged. "It is a business, Salome. A very lucrative one."

Salome nodded slowly, before rising from her chair. "I understand, Don." Reaching over, she ran a hand over the top of the smooth skin on Tomas' head and bent down to place a soft kiss on it, before saying, "I'm going to go to upstairs now."

He nodded, the look on his face guarded as he watched her closely.

Turning, she walked away, pausing and glancing back when she reached the hallway. "Tomas?"

"Yeah?"

"Earlier, you said you had two reasons to find Diego, and one to live." Salome hesitated before asking, "What is your reason for living?"

A slow smile crossed his face, and the look in his eyes softened somewhat. "You."

Her breath hitched in her throat, and she gave a small nod. Then, with one last look at the man she was quickly falling for, she left the room.

"Is she going to be okay?" she heard Javier ask in concern. She didn't wait around to hear the reply. She knew the answer already. Right now, she just needed some time and space to process everything she learned. Her family smuggled guns, the man she cared for was in to drug smuggling, the person after her had killed Tomas' mother and now wanted Salome. It was all too much.

Salome opened the door to her bedroom and slipped inside, fighting back tears as she struggled to find the answers to several questions that plagued her. How had she not realized the kind of things her family was in to? How had she missed it? And then there was Tomas. Could she live with a man who was not only a part of the mafia, but who made and sold drugs that were probably taking the lives of men, women, and children across the country? A man who admitted that he had killed. It would seem she had a lot to learn about regarding the new world she'd found herself in.

Sighing, Salome ran a hand through her hair, walking over to lie down on the bed. She was such a hypocrite. Here she was asking herself if she could live with Tomas knowing he'd taken lives, when she planned on confronting Diego Valdez herself and putting a bullet in his heart, if she could get close enough. Just because she'd never done it before, didn't mean she never would. Not if pushed hard enough.

"Tomas," she whispered his name, letting her eyelids drift shut as sleep overcame her. She never saw the man who entered her room. Never felt him next to her as he stared down at her, raking his gaze over her body as she laid on top of the covers. Never felt the needle that he slid into her skin, depressing something in her that would ensure she didn't wake up for several hours. Never knowing that he lifted her up after dropping an envelope on the end table by her bed addressed to Tomas, and left the room through the balcony door, the same way he had come in.

CHAPTER ELEVEN

"I can go for you this time, Tomas," Javier offered, after going over the specs of the villa with him. "Stay with Salome. She needs you now."

"I agree, Son," Miguel said, reaching over to place a hand on Tomas' shoulder. "The only way to make a relationship work is to be in it one hundred percent. Stay home. Talk it out with Salome. Let one of your brothers scout out the area and report back to us."

"She wants to go with me," Tomas said quietly, every bone in his body protesting the thought.

"She what?" Miguel asked, shaking his head. "Why the hell would she want to do that? She came to us for protection. Now, she needs to let us keep her safe."

Sighing, Tomas rubbed a hand over his head, then down his face. "She asked for protection until she could find out who was after her, Papá. Now she knows, and we basically handed her the way to find him. My Salome is a strong, independent woman. She thinks she will be able to track him down and confront him herself."

"And what? Put a bullet in him?"

"She does know how to use a gun," Javier put in, his gaze moving back to his laptop.

"But she's never killed before?"

"No," Tomas said, "and I don't want her to ever know what it's like. She's better than that—better than me."

"We all like to think that about our women, Son, but the truth is, they are stronger than any of us. If someone threatens the ones they love, they will do whatever needs to be done to protect them."

"He threatened her brothers," Javier said. "While her father is a piece of shit, she loves her brothers. You could see that plain as day when she was talking to them on the phone last week. She will kill for them, there is no doubt in my mind. Not only that, but I don't think they are the only ones she will be thinking about if the opportunity arises."

"What do you mean?" Tomas demanded, fear running through him at the thought of the woman he hoped to make his, trying to take on someone like Valdez.

"Diego killed your mother, Tomas," Javier said quietly, glancing over to meet his gaze. "Did you see the look on her face when she heard that? Salome Villanueva loves you, man. I can see it, even if you can't. I've spent a little time with her since she's been here. Just at dinners, but we've talked. I get the impression that woman would walk through fire for someone she cares about. And right now, that someone is you."

"She doesn't really know me," Tomas protested, even though the same could be said for him. The feelings he had for her were very strong.

"She knows you through us," Miguel said quietly. "Your mother and I have spent every night with her, telling her about you and your brothers. She knows you more than you think."

"Fuck."

"The love of a good woman is nothing to curse over," his father reprimanded.

"It is if it could get her killed," Tomas countered, rising from his chair.

"Where are you going?"

"To check on Salome," Tomas told them, as he stalked from the kitchen.

He went to the library first, remembering she wanted to get a different book to read, but she wasn't there. He wasted no time making his way down the hall to her bedroom and pounding on the door. "Salome! It's Tomas." When there was no response, he tried again, "Salome, open the door. We need to talk."

He waited a moment, but when there was still no reply, he tried the door. The knob turned in his hand and the door opened, showing him an empty room. Crossing to the bathroom, he glanced inside to find it empty as well. The balcony door was shut, and there was no sign of anyone outside.

"Salome?"

Where the hell was she? She said she was coming upstairs. Did she go to his room? That wouldn't make sense, though. It was all the way on the other side of the villa, and she'd never been there before. He didn't know if she even knew the way.

He glanced over at the bed again, and his eyes narrowed on the slight impression he could see on the comforter. An outline of her body. The bed had obviously been made after he left it this morning, so that would mean that she had come back here and laid down after their conversation. Right?

That's when Tomas noticed the envelope with his name on it sitting on the end table. His heart caught in his throat at the thought of what it could be. A note telling him good-bye? Did she leave? After everything he trusted her with, after he let her in further than anyone else besides his family, she walked out on him.

Pain swamped him, surging through him like a volcano, and before he knew it, he was striking out, putting a fist through the wall in front of him. *She left. She fucking left him.*

"Tomas, what in the world is going on?"

He heard Sofia's voice through his rage, but he couldn't reply. He let another fist fly, pounding into the wall beside the bed. He was aware of Sofia screaming for his father, but he couldn't stop.

"Where is Salome?" his father's voice thundered through the room. "Who took her?"

"She left," Tomas bit out. "She's gone."

"She would not have just left you, Tomas," Sofia argued. "There's no way."

"She's gone!" he hollered again, dropping to the bed and cradling his head in his hands.

Then Mateo was next to him, reaching for the note and opening it. Reading it.

"Fuck! She didn't leave you. Diego has her."

The words reached Tomas when nothing else could, and he swung around to face his brother. "What the fuck are you talking about?"

"She didn't walk out of here on her own free will,

Tomas." Glancing down at the note in his hand, Mateo read,

Tomas,

Son of my brother's deceitful wife. I have spies everywhere. I've been watching you for years, toying with the idea of when I would kill you and how. It was never a question of if it would happen. The second I found out you were a De La Vega, I knew you were dead. I was content to wait, but then you had to go and mess in my business. I knew the second Salome Villanueva showed up at your front gate. Still, I decided to wait. To give her father a few more days to repay me, even though I planned on claiming her afterwards, anyway. Then you made a mistake, Tomas. You touched what is mine, and for that, you will both die. However, her death will be much slower and more painful than yours. They do call me Devil for a reason. I have no heart, no soul, and no moral code I live by. Salome will soon find that out.

Devil Diego

Tomas grabbed the letter from his brother and read it again, and then again. She hadn't left him. She'd been taken, which was even worse. If she'd left him, it would have gutted him, but he would have continued on. Knowing she was alive would have been what mattered. If Diego followed through with his threat, killing her in the process, he didn't think he would survive.

"We have a traitor in our house," Sofia whispered. "Who could it be, Javier? You have looked into the background of everyone here. Which one of them would turn on us? If you find them, we can find Salome."

Tomas froze at his mother's words, a cold, hard grin of anticipation crossing his face. She was right. Someone that had access to their household had to be on Diego's payroll. If they found the traitor, the chances of them finding Salome in time were greater.

"How do we play this?" Javier asked. "I can dig into every background here. Their online accounts, cell phone records, whatever it takes, but I don't think we have time for that."

"You have the villa that you found. We can look into it," his father contemplated, walking over to the balcony doors and staring outside. "We should send someone there."

"Contact her brothers. Have one of them check out the villa," Javier suggested. "It's closer to them than it is to us."

"Done," Mateo said, picking up his cell phone. "I'll call Kain."

"Pull up a list of all employees that have access to our home," Miguel ordered. "We will go through them one-by-one."

"There is no need for that." Tomas looked over to see Luciana Reyes standing in the doorway, tears of anger in her eyes as she held the arm of a young female tightly. Giving her a shove. Luciana sent the woman tumbling into the room, falling to her knees on the carpet. "Tell them! You tell them what you did to our Salome!"

Tomas recognized her as Marisol Gomez, someone who had worked for them for several years now. She came to them with no money and nowhere to go. They'd taken her in, fed her, clothed her, and given her a job. And this was how she repaid them?

Marisol glared up at Luciana mutinously sneering, "She is not *our* anything. She belongs to Diego and now he has her back!"

"That is where you are very wrong," Sofia said quietly, stepping forward before Tomas could. "Salome belongs to my son, Tomas, which makes her a part of this familia."

"I overheard her on the phone telling someone she was paid a lot of money to hand over Salome to Diego," Luciana spat out. "She told them she opened the balcony door on Salome's bedroom to let the enemy in. That she was to go lock it again afterwards but hadn't made it back up just yet."

Miguel reached out and pushed the handle down on the door, and they all watched as it swung open easily. Salome would not have made that mistake. She knew she was allowed to go out on the balcony whenever she wanted, but was to always lock up again when she came back inside. Not only for her safety, but for that of the entire familia. There was no way she would have left it unlocked. The Don slowly turned around to look at Marisol where she still knelt on the floor. "What you have done is not acceptable in my household. There will be severe reper-cussions."

"They will be worth it," Marisol said, laughing wildly.

Tomas reached for the gun he kept at his back, but he wasn't quick enough. To his surprise, Sofia was faster. Stepping forward, she grabbed the woman by her hair as she pulled a knife from a sheath hidden at her ankle and put it swiftly to Marisol's throat. "You will tell us where they have taken Salome," she ordered, the knife drawing blood as it bit into Marisol's skin.

"Fuck you."

"You will tell us, now!" Sofia spat out, "or after I am done with you, I will go after all of whom you love. Don't think I won't. My son is very good at weeding out information on the internet, and I know for a fact that you've been seeing someone lately."

Marisol's eyes widened, then narrowed on her. "No, I haven't. You don't know what you are talking about."

"I know more than you think, woman. This is my familia. It is my business to know."

"A young male, twenty-three years old," Javier barked out from where he now sat in a chair by the balcony, his laptop open on his lap. "Brown hair, brown eyes, six foot three. Lives an hour from here, and by the looks of it, I would say he has no idea that you've sold out to Valdez." Raising his head to meet her gaze, he said, "Or that you currently work for the mafia. I'm assuming the rest of his family doesn't either. A mother and two little sisters. Do I need to go on?"

"He means nothing to me," she whispered, even though her chin began to wobble slightly.

Glancing back down at the computer screen, Javier's fingers slipped across the keyboard before he said, "Oh, that's right, you have no family… except for your grandmother who is in a nursing home with Alzheimer's. You tried to keep her a secret from us for some reason, which I never understood, until just now when I found out you work for the Devil. She is an hour and a half away." Looking at his watch, he grinned over at Mateo, "Bet I could make it there in twenty."

"I'll take that bet," Mateo muttered, his eyes on the girl.

"No," Tomas said, crossing his arms over his chest as he stared at Marisol unemotionally. "She took Salome from me. She sent her to Valdez, who will use her, abuse her, break her, and then kill her. Salome is mine, which means I will be going to her grandmother first. Then, her boyfriend and his family. Then, once I do find Salome, Marisol will suffer double every single thing my woman has before she dies."

Marisol looked over at him and gulped, terror in her eyes. Anyone who knew Tomas knew he didn't play games. If he said he was going to do something, he did it. When he started for the door, she cried out, "No! Please! I will tell you where she is." When he just kept walking, she whispered out an address, her voice clogged with tears.

Tomas stopped, turning to look at his brother, relief filling him when after a moment Javier threw a fist into the air. "Yes! That son of a bitch is only an hour from here."

"It's valid?" Sofia asked.

"As far as I can tell."

"Good," she said, right before she slid her blade across Marisol's throat, and then dropped her lifeless body to the floor. "Go, get Salome and bring her home."

"Holy shit, Mamá," Javier said, his eyes glued to the woman who was bleeding out all over the light-colored carpet.

"No one messes with my familia," Sofia snapped before motioning toward Luciana. "Clean up this mess, please."

"With pleasure," Luciana said, glaring down at the body before walking over to kick it with her small foot.

Glancing up at Tomas, she said, "You go get Salome. My Raul will take care of this problem for you." When he raised an eyebrow in question, she shrugged. "I hear things around here. I know that you are the cleaner when something like this happens. You have more important things to worry about right now. Raul has gotten rid of more than one body in his lifetime. One more won't make a difference."

"Well, shit," Mateo muttered, shaking his head. "Who exactly did you work for before coming here?"

"You don't want to know," Javier said, rising from his chair and heading for the door that Tomas was already walking through. "Let's go get Salome."

"What about her brothers?" Miguel asked as he followed them down the hall.

"Let them go to the villa on the off chance that Marisol told us wrong," Tomas shot back. "Meet out front in ten minutes. I'm grabbing some things from my room. If you are there when I get out, I'll take you with me. If not, you find your own way."

"You forget, dickhead, I'm the one with the address," Javier said, following him down a set of stairs to get to his suites in the villa.

"You already shared that information," Tomas reminded him. "Ten minutes."

CHAPTER TWELVE

S alome groaned as she struggled to open her eyes. Her head was pounding, and her mouth was so dry it tasted like cotton. Groaning again, she reached up to rub her face and found she couldn't move her arms. Trying one more time, she froze when she realized she was stuck, her wrists tied down to something.

"Let Diego know she's awake."

It was a voice she didn't recognize, and it sent a shiver of terror down her spine.

"What's he going to do with her?" a female voice asked timidly.

"That is none of your concern, Alejandra. Now, go!"

"Yes, Sir."

Salome managed to pry her eyes open just enough so that she could look around groggily. Everything was blurry at first, but after a moment it began to appear clearer. She felt weak, her body heavy.

Moving her head to the side, she blinked several times as she tried to focus on what was going on around her. She was in a small room, laying down on a twin-sized bed. She could see a man standing a few feet away with his back to her. He was messing with something on a small tray, but she couldn't see what. She wasn't sure she wanted to. She'd seen movies that started out like this, and they always ended badly.

The door opened again, and a young woman stepped inside. Salome could make out light brown hair that fell to her shoulders, a slim build, and it looked like she was dressed in jeans and a dark, long-sleeved shirt. When she moved closer, Salome had to smother a gasp at the sad, golden-brown eyes tinged with fear that stared back at her. They seemed to seal her fate already.

"I called him, Uncle. He said he is busy and will be here when he gets here."

The man turned around and frowned at her. "Did he say when that might be?"

"No, but he said to wait for him."

The man huffed, shaking his head as he crossed the room to stare down at Salome. His small, beady eyes behind wide, wire-rimmed glasses would have been comical, except there was nothing funny about her situation. "Well, you stay with her, then. I have a few things I need to do. If he shows before I get back, holler."

"Yes, Sir."

Salome waited until the door shut behind the man before she rasped, "Please, can I have some water?"

The woman hesitated, looking over to the door, then held a finger up to her lips. Salome watched as she moved quietly across the room to where a small fridge sat, retrieved a bottle of water, and came back. After another look at the door, she took the lid off and slid an arm under Salome's neck to help her sit up a little, then put the water to her lips. Salome drank small sips in silence, knowing the woman was taking a risk helping her, not wanting to get her in trouble. Soon, she was being lowered back down, and the excess water wiped from her mouth.

"Alejandra?" she whispered. "That's your name?"

Alejandra nodded, tears clouding her eyes. "I'm so sorry," she whispered, so softly Salome almost couldn't hear her. "I would get you out of here if I could, but this place is huge. I've only been here a couple of weeks and have no idea where I'm going if I leave this wing of the building."

"It's all right," Salome replied, and she meant it. She didn't want to put the other woman at risk any more than she already had.

"No, it isn't," Alejandra whispered. "I don't know what they are planning on doing to you, but it isn't good. They've had two people in this room before you, and neither one made it out alive."

"Just talk to me," Salome said softly. "Take my mind off of things."

"Okay, I can do that," Alejandra said, glancing over at the door again. "Let's see, my name is Alejandra Sanchez. I moved here with my uncle a couple of weeks ago after my parents died." She shrugged, "I had no choice. I didn't have anywhere else to go, and he sent men to our apartment who brought me here."

"I can relate," Salome said sardonically, glancing over at her shackled wrist.

"Um, my father was a policeman and my mother stayed home and raised me and my older sister, Valeria.

She's married and lives in the United States now with her husband and two children."

"Maybe you can go live with them?" Salome suggested, closing her eyes as she thought of her own mother's absence, along with a father who didn't care for her.

"She wouldn't want that," Alejandra said quietly. "She left us behind on purpose."

Deciding not to pry, Salome asked, "How old are you, Alejandra?"

She seemed so young and inexperienced that Salome was surprised when she said, "I'll be twenty-four next month."

Twenty-four, and stuck with a man like Diego, possibly for the rest of her life? Of course, Salome could be right there with Alejandra, but it was more likely that death was what waited for her.

Unless Tomas came for her. Hope began to seep in at that thought. He had said she was his reason for living. That meant he cared for her, right? Would he come?

The door opened, and Salome heard someone come into the small room, but she kept her eyes closed as if she were asleep.

"Alejandra, what are you doing with that water?"

"I was thirsty, Sir. I hope that's okay?"

"As long as that is all you were doing, young lady?"

"What else would I do with it but drink it?" Alejandra asked, the bewilderment in her voice believable.

Salome opened her eyes just enough to see the man shake his head in exasperation. "Diego called again. It is going to be at least an hour before he is here. I have to step out for a while. I'm leaving you in charge of our… prisoner… while I'm out." He paused before saying, "Do not mess this up, Alejandra, or you will not live through the repercussions. Diego Valdez is not an understanding man."

"Yes, Uncle," Alejandra rasped, her voice full of terror.

"I mean it, Alejandra. Do not mess this up for me."

"Yes, Sir."

After he left the room, Alejandra walked over to a wooden chair that sat beside a small desk and lowered herself into it. Her hands were shaking, and she accidentally dropped the bottle of water on the floor. "What the hell is going on? Who are these crazy ass people?"

Slowly letting her eyes open all the way, Salome whispered, "You don't know?"

Alejandra shook her head, shoving her hands into her hair as she stared at Salome in despair. "I haven't seen my uncle since I was a child, and I never heard the name Diego Valdez until I arrived here. I met him once." Ducking her head, she said, "He's evil—pure evil." She was quiet for a moment, then asked, "Who are you?"

Salome didn't know why, but she trusted Alejandra. Maybe it was naïve of her, but she did all the same, so she replied with the truth. "I am Salome Villanueva, daughter of Fabio Villanueva, the man who tried to give me to Diego to pay off a debt he owes. Instead, I ran."

"Oh?"

"Yep. My father is an asshole, just like everyone else here."

"Where did you go?"

"To the mafia to beg for their help."

"The mafia?!"

"The De La Vega famalia in Cali," Salome told her softly.

"They are actually wonderful people, Alejandra. They took me in, kept me safe." She laughed ruefully, "Well, as safe as they could up until now, but they did the best they could."

"Do you think…" Alejandra glanced toward the door before lowering her voice. "Do you think they will come for you, Salome?"

"I hope so," Salome whispered, letting her eyes close again, "otherwise, I am a dead woman."

There was a rustle of movement, and suddenly Alejandra was by her side. "I can't let that happen. I would never forgive myself."

Salome watched in surprise as Alejandra used a knife she held tightly to cut through the bonds that tied Salome to the bed. Then, she slipped a hand under Salome's shoulders and urged her to sit up. Dizziness swamped her, and she moaned, her hand going to her head that was beginning to ache. All after affects of whatever drug they'd given her when she was knocked out at home, she was sure.

"Hurry, we have to get moving."

"But I thought you didn't know where to go?"

"I know exactly two ways out of this place," Alejandra told her. "The door they brought me through, and a body bag. I prefer the first way. You?"

Salome nodded slowly, her eyes narrowing on the younger woman. "You don't think this is going to work, do you? That's why you refused to do it before."

"No, I don't," Alejandra said honestly, "but I can't just sit here and watch you die."

"Alejandra, if they catch us, your fate will be the same as mine."

Alejandra's eyes clouded over, but she whispered, "I would rather share your fate than watch you live it."

Salome squeezed her eyes shut tightly, then swung her legs over the side of the bed. "Let's do this then."

They had just stumbled to the door, Alejandra's arm around Salome's waist as she practically carried her across the room, when it opened revealing the uncle on the other side. His head was down as he looked at some documents in his hands, and Alejandra moved so quickly Salome had to fight to stay standing. One moment the girl was holding her up, the next she was slamming the side of a lamp into his head. Groaning, he slid to the floor as he lost consciousness.

"Shit! Let's go!"

Wrapping her arm around Salome's waist again, Alejandra urged her out of the room and down a hall. They'd made it to the end and Alejandra was pushing her to go right, when there was a loud commotion outside the door at the end of the hallway they were heading into.

"This way," Salome hissed, pulling out of Alejandra's grip and grabbing her hand as they moved in the other direction. The fog was slowly clearing from her head and she was able to move on her own, just not too fast.

They came to a set of double doors, and Salome pushed them open, stumbling through, then stopped abruptly. There, on the other side, stood all three of her brothers with guns raised and pointed in her direction.

"Uh oh," Alejandra whispered, coming to a dead stop as she stared at them. "Now what?"

Her eyes welled up with tears and they spilled over, flowing down her cheeks as she whispered, "Now, we go home."

"Fuck, Sis," Kain said, shaking his head as he lowered his rifle, "you really know how to worry a man, don't ya?"

Before she could reply, she felt someone slam into her, knocking her to the floor as the loud sound of gunfire filled the room. The person on top of her grunted as their body jerked more than once, and then as soon as the gunfire started, it stopped.

"Salome! Dammit, Salome, answer me!"

She could hear Giovanni screaming for her, but her ears were ringing and no matter how hard she tried, she couldn't answer. Pain lanced through her left arm, and the body on top of her wasn't moving, which meant she couldn't move.

Suddenly, they were there. Her brothers. Her saviors. They lifted the body off of her, laying it gently on the floor beside her. She cried out when she saw who it was. "No! Alejandra! No! Please!"

The woman laid on her back, blood pooling around her from numerous bullet wounds. Her hair fanned out around her on the cold, white linoleum that was quickly staining a dark red color. Her mouth opened slightly as she stared at Salome. "Are we going home now, Salome?" she rasped, as tears fell from the corners of her eyes. Alejandra's body began to shake, her breath coming hard and fast as she whispered again, "Home?"

Salome cupped her face in her hands, a sob catching in her throat as she rasped, "Yeah, sweet girl. We're going home."

"Tell me about it," Alejandra whispered, as shivers racked her body.

"The medic will be here any minute," Kain said

gruffly, kneeling beside them. "Keep her talking, Salome, while I do what I can to stop the bleeding."

Salome nodded, locking her eyes with the other woman's as she told her, "Home is so beautiful, Alejandra, with acres and acres of trees surrounding our villa. There's a gardener who takes care of the lawn and he has stunning flowers all around." Salome ignored her brother's look of confusion he had sent her way. She was describing *her* home, not his. "The house is gorgeous, all hardwood floors with these stunning area rugs Sofia loves that are laid down everywhere. And our familia is amazing. They are loyal to a fault."

"I love them already," Alejandra breathed, her eyes slowly drifting closed as a soft smile spread across her face.

"Miguel is the Don," Salome went on, stroking the woman's hair back gently. "He is very good to us, even though he can be hard when he needs to be. And Sofia, the Mamá, she is so kind and giving. No one could ask for a better mother. Tomas, my man, would walk through fire to save the ones he cares about. He is gruff, and short on words, but has a big heart. Although, he would never want anyone to know."

"Sounds wonderful."

Salome was aware of Gio kneeling next to them holding his phone, but she didn't take her gaze from the woman in front of her. "Mateo is another one of the brothers. He is very strong and is the second to the Don. One day, he will lead the familia, but right now he watches and learns."

"Smart," Alejandra rasped, a soft moan of pain escaping. "I like smart."

"Yes, he is very smart, handsome too." Alejandra tried to smile, but it seemed like a weak attempt. "I think you would like Javier the best," Salome went on softly.

"Yeah?"

"Oh, yes. He is closet to your age, and he is a computer genius. He spends a lot of time on his laptop, and I swear he can do anything on that thing." Salome could hear sirens in the background, and she gently stroked the hair back away from Alejandra's forehead again. "He's very funny and loves to tease. And, he has a soft side that he tries to hide, but I've seen it. He loves his family, especially his mother."

"Good man."

"One of the best," Salome agreed.

"Will they like me?" Alejandra gasped, more tears slipping from the corners of her eyes.

"You saved my life, sweet girl. They will love you. I already do, and I just met you."

"Hurts."

Salome's heart clenched, and she lowered her head down near Alejandra's. "I know it does. I would take your pain from you if I could."

"They're turning in now, Salome," Kain said quietly.

"Your brother?" Alejandra whispered.

"Yes, this is Kain; Dario and Gio, my other brothers, are here, too."

"Never had a brother. I think I would like one."

"You have to back up now, Sis. They're here."

Salome grasped Alejandra's hand tightly, as she promised, "I'll be at the hospital when you wake up! Then, we'll go home, Alejandra. I promise!"

Alejandra's eyes closed, and Salome heard one last

word before Kain pulled her away from where the medics were fighting to bring the girl back to life. "Home."

"I need to call Tomas," Salome said woodenly, as she watched Alejandra fight for her life. "I need to tell him…" She paused, unsure what to say. She wanted to tell Tomas that she loved him, needed him, didn't want to live without him. She didn't care if he was the son of a Don who smuggled drugs for a living and killed when he had to. All she cared about was him and the man she knew he was. "I need him," she finally said, glancing over at her brothers.

"He knows, Sis," Gio said, slipping an arm around her waist after handing his phone over to Dario. "He's a bit busy right now, but as soon as he's done, he will find you. I promise."

"Busy doing what?" Salome whispered, her eyes going back to Alejandra.

"Preparing for the future," Gio said solemnly, his gaze following hers.

CHAPTER THIRTEEN

"Holy shit," Javier said, his eyes meeting Tomas' while he clutched the phone he held tightly. "That girl better not fucking die. Not after she just saved Salome's life."

Tomas agreed silently, knowing he would be forever grateful to Alejandra, whoever she was. If she made it, he would make sure she never lacked for anything. She would have the home she seemed to desperately crave, with him and his family.

"She claimed our home as hers," Mateo said quietly. "Her brothers are right there with her, but our home is the one she described to Alejandra."

"And us," Javier whispered.

"Because we are her familia now," Miguel said roughly, taking the phone from his youngest son. Putting it to his ear, he demanded, "What of our Salome? Is she safe? Is she hurt?" He listened for a moment, then said, "We need to take care of business here, and then we will come for her. You do not leave her side, or you will answer to me, Don De La Vega, you understand?" Without waiting for a response, he hung up the phone and handed it back to Javier. "Now, let's take care of business so we can get back home to our familia. They need us."

"Wait, what of Salome?" Tomas asked, needing to hear for himself that she was safe.

"She will be fine, my son. A bullet grazed her arm, which someone is looking at now, but Alejandra took the brunt of it. We all owe that young lady a debt that we may never be able to repay. Not if she doesn't make it out of the hospital."

"Looks like they are getting ready to move out, Don," one of their men called out. "If we are going to take them, we need to move now."

Miguel looked at his sons and they all nodded in agreement. They wasted no time piling into the vehicles and taking off down the road that would lead them to the house they were positive Diego Valdez was still at. It didn't take long, and soon they, along with twenty-five of their best men, were surrounding the small villa.

Tomas clipped two of the men as he leaped out of the jeep he was in, managing to get a third as he raced around to the back of the house, knowing that was where Diego would emerge. The fucking coward. He was right. He'd just rounded the corner when the bastard ran out the back door and down a path toward a forest of trees, leaving his men behind to fight without him. Raising his gun, Tomas pointed and fired, hitting the Devil in his left leg.

Diego stumbled, but managed to keep going. Tomas fired again, hitting the other leg, deliberately aiming to hurt, not kill.

"Son of a bitch!" Diego screamed as he fell to the

ground, rolling onto his back and clutching his legs in agony.

Trusting his brothers and men to take care of the others, Tomas focused on Diego, stalking over to him and staring silently down. Diego flinched when his gaze met Tomas', and Tomas knew it was because the man saw death in his eyes.

Pointing the Glock again, Tomas pulled the trigger, a satisfied grin crossing his face when he put a bullet in Diego's hand. "This is a disappointment," he drawled, staring down at the man who had been bigger than life in a little boy's nightmares. Now, he was nothing but an old, fat piece of shit. He was nothing without his men to back him.

"Fuck you, you little illegitimate bastard."

Tomas chuckled without humor. "Is that the best you got, Diego? Cause, from where I'm standing, those words don't mean shit."

"You, De La Vega scum!"

Tomas raised his gun again, narrowing his eyes on Diego. "As much as I would love to draw this out since it's all I've dreamt of ever since you killed my mother, I can't. My woman needs me. I gotta go."

"You have no woman. Salome is mine. I own her."

"Kind of hard to own something when you are dead, asshole," Javier drawled coming up behind Tomas. "All these dumbasses are gone, brother. Can you hurry this up? We need to get to Salome."

"You won't get any argument from me," Tomas said, right before putting a bullet between the eyes of the fucker who haunted his woman's dreams. "That was for my mother."

Mateo walked over to them, staring down at Diego for

a moment, before saying, "He doesn't seem so dark and dangerous in person, does he?"

A short burst of laughter left Tomas as he agreed, "Nope, not at all."

"Ready to get out of here, brother?"

Tomas nodded, before aiming the gun at Diego's sad excuse for a cock and pulling the trigger. "That was for Salome, and this, Motherfucker, is for me!" He took another shot, this time striking the Devil in his cold, dead heart. A perfect end to his evil reign that had imprisoned Tomas for so many years. Tomas blamed Diego for making his heart turn cold years ago, not knowing if it would ever beat again. Then he met Salome. She brought him back to life, making his heart beat with a vigorous, renewed spirit—one that only a woman like her could create. He stood there for a moment, taking in the aftermath of killing his long-time nemesis. It was oddly too easy, and the rage inside his heart still lingered, even though the man was now dead. It wasn't until he thought of Salome waiting for him at the hospital, the image of holding her in his arms and kissing those lips of seduction, that the pressure and vengeance he felt inside his chest was finally freed. His future was waiting for him back home, while his past laid on the cold ground, bleeding out for all the sins he created.

"We can go now, Brothers, Salome needs me."

CHAPTER FOURTEEN

Tomas took one last look around his bedroom, nervous anticipation running through him. He'd never done anything like this before. Hell, he'd never even brought a woman to the villa, let alone decked out his room in candles and had dinner brought up to share with her. He wasn't lying when he told Salome he was a one-night stand type of guy. He never let anyone get too close. He had a lot of enemies that could use his woman to their advantage if they wanted to. He lost his mother to this life and had no desire to lose a spouse. But he found with Salome he couldn't walk away. So, instead, he was going to push forward and do whatever he had to do to keep her safe.

It had been two months since he took Diego out. Two months since he almost lost the woman he claimed as his. If it wasn't for Alejandra Sanchez, he would have. Instead, the young woman was now in a coma, fighting for her life at the hospital. Salome went every day to see her, and he knew for a fact she wasn't the only one. Every single person in their family stopped by at least twice a week, if not more. Salome told them Alejandra had no one else, so his family did what they did best, absorbed her into their own.

Since then, he'd been taking the time to get to know Salome. Her likes and dislikes, her favorite food, movie, color, anything he could find out about her. And he had to admit, over that time he'd lost his heart to her.

There was a soft knock on his door, and he quickly crossed the room to open it. Sofia stood there, a gentle smile on her face and a small box in her hand.

"Mamá, I thought you and the familia were going out to dinner?"

"We are," she said, her gaze going beyond him to where the room was lit by soft candlelight. "You did good, my son."

He gave her a boyish smile and a shrug. "I hope she likes it."

"Your Salome will love it," Sofia said, before holding out the box to him. "I wanted to give this to you, Tomas. It was my grandmother's. When you are ready, I hope you will give it to the woman you choose to join with."

Tomas noticed how she refrained from saying Salome's name, even though they already knew who his choice was. Taking the box from her, he opened it to find a dark blue velvet ring box inside. Slowly, he opened the lid, and swallowed hard when he saw the large diamond inside.

"She was buried with her wedding band, but it is tradition in my familia to pass the engagement ring down to the first-born son when we believe he is ready."

Tomas' heart clenched in his chest as he raised his head

to meet Sofia's gaze. "I love it, Mamá, but shouldn't this go to Mateo?"

"Last time I checked, Mateo was not my eldest son," Sofia said, reaching up to place the palm of her hand against his cheek. "You are mine, Tomas De La Vega. I claimed you the day your father brought you home to me. I love you just as much as I do my other sons. The ring belongs to you."

Tomas took a deep breath and wrapped his arms tightly around her, holding her close. "Thank you, Mamá. I love you, too." It was the first time he had said those words to her since he was a child. It wasn't that he didn't feel it, but he wasn't one to share his emotions with anyone—not even family.

Sofia held him back tightly, patting his back the way she did years ago. "I love you too, Mijo." They stayed like that for several moments before she whispered, "Now, go find that woman of yours. Be good to her. Treat her with the love and respect she deserves."

"Yes, Mamá." He didn't tell her about the ring he had already purchased for Salome. It was sitting on his dresser, ready to be given to her that night. No, that ring would be going back, because this ring meant so much more. He understood what his father meant when he talked about the soul versus the heart. He knew he handed Salome his soul the minute their eyes met, and he was now ready to give her the rest of him.

He watched Sofia go, his heart feeling lighter than it had in a long time, before shutting the door behind him and making his way down the hall toward Salome's room. She was in a small suite on the other side of the villa, but he was hoping to change that soon. He didn't want her that far away from him anymore.

Knocking on her door, Tomas waited quietly for Salome to open it, then about swallowed his tongue when she did. A vision dressed in a dark red dress that accented the highlights in her hair, opened that door, and she was the sexiest woman he'd ever seen. He let his gaze slowly wander over her, from the dark, silky hair that flowed over her shoulders and the soft swells of her full breasts, to the luscious curves of her hips, down to the matching red high heels. The dress clung to her like a second skin, leaving nothing to the imagination, and he wondered how the hell he was going to keep his hands off her until after dinner.

Clearing his throat, he rasped, "You look beautiful, sweetheart."

A touch of dark pink tinged her cheeks as she murmured, "Thank you. Your mother took me shopping and helped me pick out the dress."

"It's perfect." He watched her face light up with joy and couldn't resist leaning down to give her a soft kiss on her dark red lips. "You ready?"

"Yes, Tomas. I've been ready," she breathed against his mouth. Her tone was low, sultry, sensuous, and had his cock standing to attention in an instant. It took all that he had to step back from her and not back her into the bedroom. As much as he wanted to, he wanted her in his bedroom more.

Slipping her hand into the crook of his elbow, Salome stepped outside her room and shut the door behind her. He slowed his steps so that they matched hers as they walked back to his suite. The second they entered; he knew he'd done something right.

"Oh, Tomas," Salome whispered, her hand going to her throat. "It's so beautiful."

His heart pounding in his chest, Tomas shut the door, and then took her hand in his. Holding it up to his lips, he gently kissed the soft skin on the back of it, his eyes locked with hers. He found that he had no patience. He couldn't wait. Right there in front of the door, he dropped to a knee, his eyes never leaving hers.

"Tomas?" Salome's eyes widened, her hand moving down to cover her heart. "What are you doing?"

Retrieving the velvet blue box from his pocket, he held it up between them. A slow smile kicked up the corners of his mouth as he said, "You own me, Salome Villanueva. My heart. My soul. All of me. I am yours, now and always. Can you accept me for who I am? What I am? Can you trust me enough to spend the rest of your life with me?"

"Oh, Tomas!" Salome breathed, dropping to her knees beside him and cupping his cheeks in her hands. "I accepted every single part of you a long time ago. I love you and will stand beside you, no matter what, forever."

"You accept, all of me?" he asked cautiously, for the first time in his life afraid of the answer.

"*All* of you," she whispered, pressing her lips to his. "You were mine the minute I laid eyes on you, Tomas De La Vega. I know who you are, in here." Salome pressed a hand over his heart. "That is what matters. Yes, I will spend the rest of my life with you—loving you."

Tomas wasted no time in opening the box and taking out the ring. It slipped on her finger as if it were made for her. "I love you, Salome," he rasped, sliding his fingers into her hair and finding her lips with his. It was a gentle kiss at first, but it had been too long since he'd been between her silky thighs—too long since he'd felt her wet heat around his cock.

When her throaty moan of pleasure reached his ears, Tomas groaned, his tongue sliding inside her mouth. Licking around the hot cavern, he found her tongue with his as his hands moved down her sides and over her legs to the hem of her dress.

"Sorry, sweetheart, your dress isn't going to stay on long."

"I hope not," she moaned, finding the front of his shirt. She started undoing his buttons, one by one, placing hot little kisses to his skin as she revealed it. "I think we are both wearing way too much clothing." Soon, she was sliding it from his shoulders, and tracing his skin with her hands.

"Fuck, Salome!"

She was licking and nibbling every part of him, and it was driving him insane.

"I've missed you, Tomas."

He chuckled, trailing kisses over the soft skin on her bare shoulder and up the side of her neck. "I've been right here with you."

"No!" Salome cried when he bit gently on her earlobe, then sucked it into his mouth. "I've missed this. You. Inside me."

Tomas had missed her too, so damn much. He hadn't touched her like this since he brought her home from the hospital. He wanted to give her time to get to know him better, be around his family, decide if life with the mafia was what she really wanted. It would have killed him to give her up, but he refused to force her into anything.

"Me too," he told her, as he urged her to her feet. "I've wanted this… you… so fucking bad."

Tomas slid her dress up her legs and then moved back so he could pull it up her body and off. He groaned at the sight of the matching red, see-through lace bra and panties set she was wearing, loving the way it played peek-a-boo with her skin. "So fucking sexy," he growled, reaching out to cup one of her breasts in his palm. Leaning down, he licked at her nipple through the lace, before sucking it into his mouth, lace and all.

"Tomas!" Salome cried, her nails digging into his chest. Sliding her hands down, she undid the buckle of his belt, along with the button and his zipper. He kicked off his shoes, and then she had his pants and boxers down and off.

When she went to kick off her heels, Tomas shook his head. "No, leave them on. I like them."

She grinned, her hand going to the front clasp of her bra. "What about this? You like it?"

"Yeah," he said hoarsely, "but it needs to go." His eyes dropped to the sexy piece of silk that covered her mound below. "All of it needs to go."

Salome laughed, undoing the clasp and slipping the bra off so her beautiful breasts hung free. Then, she slid her panties down, and she stood before him in nothing but her heels. "You like?" she whispered; her eyes bright with passion.

"I fucking love," he growled, pulling her to him and slamming his mouth down on hers. Wrapping his arm around her waist, he lifted her and carried her to the bed. Breaking the kiss, he sat her on the mattress, and then guided her back so she laid before him. Sexy, sensual, hot.

"Please, Tomas," she begged, spreading her legs, offering herself to him. "I need you."

"I'm yours." Grasping her hips, Tomas pulled her to the edge of the bed, bumping the head of his cock up against her entrance. She was soaked with need, and it coated the tip of his dick, making him bite back a groan as he slid all of the way inside. "You feel so good," he rasped, once he was as deep as he could go.

"You, too."

Tomas looked down at his woman where she laid on his bed. Her hair was spread out around her, curly and wild. Her dark green eyes glowed with pleasure as her mouth opened slightly, her lips a dark, shiny red. Her nipples were beaded up on her pert breasts, and he couldn't stop himself from leaning over and licking at one just before tugging it into his mouth. When she gasped, her hands came up to cradle his head, as he continued to stroke her with his tongue and slowly began to move inside her.

She was so tight and squeezed his cock like a glove. As much as he wanted to go slow, he couldn't. It had been too long. Salome panted his name, her little moans filling the air as she moved with him. Quickly, he let go of her nipple so that he could give the other one attention, knowing he wasn't going to last long.

"Tomas, harder! I need to feel you," Salome moaned, her hands going to his back, her nails raking across his skin. She wrapped her legs around his waist, and he could feel the tips of her heels digging in his ass.

Tomas rose up. While holding her hips, he began to pound inside her. Fast, hard, just the way she wanted it. All too soon, he felt the pressure in his balls as they began to draw up. He tried to hold back, but the feel of her hot sheath strangling his dick was just too much. Finding her clit with his thumb, he rubbed it as he slammed in and out of her.

"Salome, come for me," he ordered, knowing he was close. Just as he hoped, his woman listened, and soon he was following her over the edge, shouting her name as he exploded inside her. He continued to move in and out of her until every last drop was wrung from him, and then he collapsed on top of her, breathing heavily.

They stayed like that for several minutes, before he finally pulled away and went to get something to clean them up with. But, instead of going to eat the dinner that was waiting for them, he picked her up and laid her on a pillow at the top of the bed, crawling in beside her and pulling her close.

Her hand rested on his chest, over the cross that she always seemed to gravitate to. Her thumb stroking gently over it. "It was my birth mother's," he said gruffly, his hand going up to cover hers, but not moving it. "It's the only thing I have of hers."

"It's beautiful," she said softly, tilting her head up to place a kiss on his chin.

"It's protected me all of these years," he told her, before letting her go and slowly reaching up to slip it away from his neck.

"Tomas?"

"Now, it will protect the woman I love," he said softly, as he slipped it around Salome's neck, hooking the clasp.

Tears filled her eyes as she whispered, "Are you sure?"

"The ring you wear is from my Mamá," Tomas said, taking her hand in his and placing a kiss over the solitaire on her finger. "The necklace is from my birth mother." Leaning down, he kissed the cross.

Salome nodded slowly, a tremulous smile appearing, telling him that she understood what he was trying to say, even if he didn't have the eloquent words to say it.

"I will treasure them both always."

"You will always hold my heart and soul in your hands, Salome Villanueva."

"As you will mine."

Mateo: Book 2 of the De La Vega Familia Trilogy
Coming April 20, 2021
mybook.to/Mateo

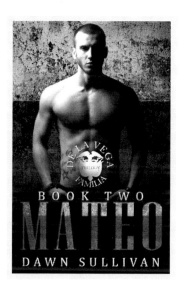

A NOTE FROM THE AUTHOR

Make sure and visit my website for information on all of my books, and to sign up for my Newsletter where you will receive all of the latest information on new releases, sales, and more!

Website: **http://www.dawnsullivanauthor.com/**

I would love to have you join my reader's group, Author Dawn Sullivan's Rebel Readers, so that we can hang out and chat, and where you will also get sneak peeks of cover reveals, read excerpts before anyone else, and more!

https://www.facebook.com/groups/AuthorDawnSulli-vansRebelReaders/

ABOUT THE AUTHOR

Dawn Sullivan has a wonderful, supportive husband, and three beautiful children. She enjoys spending time with them, which normally involves some baseball, shooting hoops, taking walks, watching movies, and reading.

Her passion for reading began at a very young age and only grew over time. Whether she was bringing home a book from the library or sneaking one of her mother's romance novels to read by the light in the hallway when she was supposed to be sleeping, Dawn always had a book. She reads several different genres and subgenres, but Paranormal Romance and Romantic Suspense are her favorites.

Dawn has always made up stories of her own, and finally decided to start sharing them with others. She hopes everyone enjoys reading them as much as she enjoys writing them.

ALSO BY DAWN SULLIVAN

RARE Series

Book 1 Nico's Heart

Book 2 Phoenix's Fate

Book 3 Trace's Temptation

Book 4 Saving Storm

Book 5 Angel's Destiny

Book 6 Jaxson's Justice

Book 7 Rikki's Awakening

White River Wolves Series

Book 1 Josie's Miracle

Book 2 Slade's Desire

Book 3 Janie's Salvation

Book 4 Sable's Fire

Serenity Springs Series

Book 1 Tempting His Heart

Book 2 Healing Her Spirit

Book 3 Saving His Soul

Book 4 A Caldwell Wedding

Book 5 Keeping Her Trust

Alluring Assassins

Book 1 Cassia

Sass and Growl

Book 1 His Bunny Kicks Sass

Book 2 Protecting His Fox's Sass

Book 3 Accepting His Witch's Sass

Book 4 Chasing His Lynx's Sass

Chosen By Destiny

Book 1 Blayke

Book 2 Bellame

Magical Mojo

Book 1 Witch Way To Love

Rogue Enforcers

Karma

Dark Leopards West Texas Chapter

Book 1 Shadow's Revenge

Book 7 Demon's Hellfire

Standalone

Wedding Bell Rock

The De La Vega Familia Trilogy (Social Rejects Syndicate)

Book 1 Tomas

Manufactured by Amazon.ca
Acheson, AB

16477351R00077